MALICE TOWARD NONE

The Kochendorfer Family in 1858-1859. Left to right: Margaret, Catherine, Johan, Jr., daughter Catherine, Johan, Sr., and Rosina. (From the collection of the Brown County Historical Society, New Ulm, Minnesota.

MALICE TOWARD NONE

Abraham Lincoln, the Civil War, the
Homestead Act, and the Massacre—and
Inspiring Survival—of the
Kochendorfers

A Minnesota History

Daniel C. Munson

North Star Press of St. Cloud, Inc.
St. Cloud, Minnesota

To Marilyn and Judy and Joe and Eileen and Nancy:
Thank you for taking the time to share with me your marvelous
family photos and stories.

ISBN: 978-0-87839- 716-7

Printed in the United States of America

Published by
North Star Press of St. Cloud, Inc.
St. Cloud, MN

www.northstarpress.com

TABLE OF CONTENTS

PROLOGUE

I COME FROM A PRACTICAL Minnesota family, and our family traditions often accomplish a number of goals at once. We're patriotic, and we observe national holidays, but not with any grand gestures. We like to exercise, but would never dream of organizing a family event around something that can be done easily enough on one's own time. So the discovery that visiting many of the family forebear's gravesites in an old cemetery near the state capital in St. Paul could be combined with a leisurely bike ride along a bike trail that passes very near my suburban house now makes for a sort of Memorial Day Weekend tradition.

Memorial Day in Minnesota is often blessed with beauty both botanic and climatic. The grass is lush and green, and often there are felt the first hints of summer warmth. The flowering fruit trees, plum and cherry and crabapple, are a little past their prime but often still brilliant. The bridal veil bushes are in full bloom, and the hydrangea that face south are already beginning to show blossoms.

There are often three generations of us on our bicycles, and we head for Oakland Cemetery, just up a short, steep hill past the trail head. Our plan is to visit and clean off a few of the stones bearing the family names, but the weather is often too nice to hurry away. The oak trees form an excellent canopy—the name of the cemetery is no misnomer—and we sometimes sit on a small hill near the cemetery chapel and sip drinks and marvel at the beauty that is springtime and the effects of over a century of patient grounds keeping.

I've hunted up a few other notable headstones at this same cemetery, the oldest cemetery in our somewhat young state, and I like to point them out and tell the stories of the semi-famous people buried there to my fellow bikers. There are the old state governors, the wealthy businessmen. The Civil War veterans have their own distinctive headstones and a reserved area.

Our family has a few descendants buried there of whom we can be proud. My paternal grandmother's grandfather was one of the state's first Methodist ministers, having arrived in St. Paul around 1860. He and his immediate family are buried along the side of a small hill that overlooks the east entrance.

I like to read the prominent headstones. The names occasionally give you a chuckle, and you're reminded of how first names are somewhat faddish: Lucius, Mathilde—these are not the names being written on today's birth certificates.

Our family forebears are mostly German—indeed, my mother biking alongside me is a German immigrant—and we enjoy some of the German family names. One year, I noticed one on a gravestone only a few dozen yards from where great-great Grandpa, Reverend Rotert, is buried: "Kochendorfer." That's a good one! I look more closely. There are three names: thirty-eight-year-old Johan, thirty-six-year-old Catherine, and three-year-old Sarah. The inscription is sad: "Victims of Redwood Falls Massacre Aug. 1862."

Here is a teachable moment! I turn to the others nearby and point to the inscription, and ask if any of my young charges can explain who or what these poor souls were victims of? One of my nieces, a shy fourteen-year-old at the time and nobody's fool, says in a soft voice: "the Indians." That's right, I tell them. Minnesota schoolchildren are often taught about the Indian Uprising of 1862 that took the lives of hundreds of the state's residents, but it takes a quick young mind to make the connection between the date and the place. I'm a bit of a history buff, but I didn't know exactly where those awful events occurred. Redwood Falls is south and west of us, along the Minnesota River, a good hundred miles away.

There were other things to concentrate on that morning. We had to agree on how much longer to stay at Oakland, because the four mile trek back home with a half-dozen young schoolchildren required a little organization. We also had to discuss which restaurant we would all go to for lunch. It was only later that the questions began to surface: What were those bodies doing there?

Nobody would have taken three dead bodies one hundred miles in 1862 just to bury them at Oakland Cemetery. How did those three unfortunate Kochendorfers get here to St. Paul? An interesting question, I thought. I wondered if there might be a good story behind it all. This book is the work of puzzling out the answer to this seemingly simple question.

The Kochendorfer Gravestone. (Courtesy of Curt Dahlin)

St. Paul, 1857.

THE ANTEBELLUM NORTH

I

RUSSIAN CZAR ALEXANDER I created a problem for himself when his soldiers drove the nomadic Tartars out of Bessarabia—the area north and east of Romania and north of the Black Sea[1]—in the early years of the nineteenth century. The Tartars hadn't been doing much with the Bessarabian soil, but now even they were gone. Russian land management being what it was, the czar had to formulate a plan. His landowning class wasn't all that interested in farming it—they had plenty of land where they were—and his serfs were incapable of organizing the effort required.

His solution was simple, and informed by the realities of European life at the time. The czar offered Bessarabian land to Germans willing to own and work it. He made them an enticing offer: zero-interest loans, religious freedom, exemption from military service, and a ten year reprieve from Russian taxes—and the Germans came.[2] A half-century before, Catherine the Great had offered land, religious freedom, and exemptions from military service to German-speaking Anabaptists—"Mennonites"—who proved good farmers, so the Russian aristocracy was comfortable with the idea of German farmers cultivating Russian soil. The Czar knew that Germany had many young people willing to apply the latest farming methods. These Germans had everything required—except farmland. The farmland in their native Germany was expensive and seldom up for sale.

1

The experiment was an early success, and tens of thousands of Germans lived on and worked the Bessarabian soil for over a century. They came primarily from southern Germany, from near the Danube River: from Bavaria, and Baden, and Wuerttemberg. They brought their Luther Bibles and their distinctive clothing and customs, but they often lived apart from the Russians, in villages that were almost exclusively German-speaking. This made them an easy target for mass deportation orders. The czar fell in 1917, and Russia lost Bessarabia to Romania in World War I, and when the Soviet Union retook it in 1940, the Bessarabian Germans were expelled by the Soviets.[3]

Nineteenth-century German farmers had other options as well. North America was being flooded with young German immigrants interested in making a better life for themselves. Many of them, like those headed for Bessarabia, were attracted by the possibilities of land ownership and farming in a New World in which their lack of capital and lack of social position would not be the huge handicaps that they were in their native Germany.

So it was that a sailing ship bound for North America in 1847 carried just such a twenty-three-year-old German named Johan Kochendorfer, who hoped to be a prosperous farmer in this New World, and another twenty-one-year-old German woman named Catherine Lechler, traveling with her sister Rosina. Johan and Catherine were both from small towns in Wuerttemberg, near Stuttgart, so they would have been able to speak to one another in the same comfortable dialect. Both sought nothing more than to try to make a go of it in America.

The two of them were married shortly after arriving.

The search for low-priced farmland often led impecunious young nineteenth-century immigrants inland, to the Ohio and Mississippi River valleys, and Johan and his young bride, Catherine, were no different. They pooled resources with her sister Rosina and her husband, Michael Ebert, and they began working a small farm in central Illinois, in Woodford County, near Peoria.

Woodford County in 1850 was an area rich in potential prosperity. The land was good for farming—Grover Cleveland's vice-president, Adlai Stevenson I of Illinois, called it some of the finest in the state—and the young Germans did well. Johan and Catherine worked the land for almost a decade, getting used to the work required, and acclimating themselves to the sweltering summers and to the long winters that were much colder and drier than anything they had known in Germany.

Catherine bore Johan five children there, the first of whom died shortly after being born in 1849. Johan, Jr., was born in 1851, then Rosina in 1853, Catherine in 1855, and Margaret in 1857. This was a real brood, a group of healthy children Johan must have considered great assets. They were also the sort of young children who might, with a little time, make good farm workers of the sort that could allow Johan to expand his farming ambitions.

These German farmers picked up English slowly, in part because they were surrounded by so many other German-speaking farmers there wasn't the pressure to learn. They were, therefore, not very interested in engaging in legal disputes conducted in English, and it does not appear the Kochendorfers had any run-ins with the law. Had they needed to resolve a legal matter of any complexity, they might have had to wait for the traveling Illinois Eighth Circuit lawyers to arrive at the Woodford County Courthouse in nearby Metamora.

One of the lawyers who made the trek to Metamora on a regular basis in the 1850s was a tall, gangly, plain-speaking fellow from the nearby state capital in Springfield. He handled many cases there, including the famous 1857 case of a Mrs. Melissa Goings, who at the age of seventy was accused of killing her husband, Roswell, after a long married life of abuse from this husband.

The lawyer met with Mrs. Goings on the first floor of the courthouse to plan their defense, and by this time it was clear some of the locals were anxious to convict her. According to courthouse legend, at one point during the discussion she told him she was thirsty, and the tall lawyer told her, "There is plenty of good drinking water in Tennessee." This lawyer turned around and left the room for a moment, and when he returned, she was gone and was never seen in Woodford County or in Illinois again, having apparently made her exit out a first floor window.[4]

That tall, gangly, plain-speaking lawyer was Abraham Lincoln. He is not known to have had any direct contact with the Kochendorfers or their relatives in Woodford County. His indirect connection to their lives, however, would be great.

II

FROM THE VERY FORMATION of the United States and even before, the people of the northern and the southern states never really got along that well. The industrious, technically-minded and business-oriented northerners thought southerners were backward, and they perhaps resented the ease and languor of southern life and wealth. The southerners found their northern brethren officious, crass, and ill-mannered. Their final blow-up concerned slavery, but they seldom saw eye-to-eye about anything.[5]

Southerners had all the decent farmland their sons could desire, and all the slaves required to work it. Northerners were more numerous, and their farmland seemed to get better as they moved west. Northern drive and ambition naturally strained the western edges of the frontier more suddenly and aggressively than in the south.

When the Kochendorfers were farming in Illinois in the 1850s it was gradually becoming evident even more such rich farmland existed just west of the Mississippi. The glaciers of the last Ice Age had pushed south, then left behind a wealth of minerals in the soil along what is now the Iowa-Minnesota border. The soil 100 miles either side of this border is almost unnaturally fertile: travelers who drive through this region today after the farmers have turned their fields over for winter or in early spring are confronted with a soil so black and rich that it almost looks as if it has been soaked in India ink.

These facts were not lost on the U.S. government. Iowa was granted statehood in 1846, and by 1860 much of the state was under cultivation, Indian land claims having been relinquished under a series of treaties. Wisconsin was granted statehood in 1848, and although Wisconsin land was somewhat more slowly developed as it was hilly and thickly wooded and did not contain the same convenient network of navigable rivers, it was clear the race was on.

The Minnesota Territory just north of Iowa and west of Wisconsin was going to be next, both for statehood and for land claims—and everybody knew it. Minnesota land was as good as that in Iowa, and three great rivers—the Mississippi, the Minnesota, and the St. Croix—made for excellent commercial transportation. President Millard Fillmore authorized his agents to begin negotiating with the Sioux—or more properly the "Dakotah," or "Lakota"[6]—Indians who lived throughout the southern half of the Territory. These Indians lived along and between the Minnesota River as it made its big loop through the Territory. The Minnesota merges with the Mississippi at Fort Snelling, just upstream and west of what in the 1850s was the burgeoning city of St. Paul.

"The Sioux," as the politically astute Episcopalian Bishop Henry Whipple of Minnesota conceded at the time, "were a warlike people."[7] They had been at war with the Chippewa, or "Ojibway," Indians of the northern part of the Minnesota Territory since time out of mind. Bishop Whipple contended, however, that "they had been our friends." One of the leaders of the Northwest Fur Company and one of the early political leaders of the Territory and later the state, Henry Sibley, is quoted by Whipple as follows: "It was a boast of the Sioux that they had never taken the life of a white man."[8]

President Fillmore and his agents believed that the Sioux were a people with whom they could, indeed they must, negotiate. The U.S. government concluded two treaties with them—the Treaty of Mendota and the Treaty of Traverse des Sioux—in which these tribes relinquished their claims to the vast area of southern Minnesota, with the exception of a "Reservation" ten miles from each side of the south-flowing section of the Minnesota River, in return for a grand total of roughly three-million dollars. The three million was to be held in trust for them by the

Bishop Henry Whipple.

5

U.S. government and interest earned at a rate of five percent per annum, the interest and some principal then paid to them once per year for fifty years. This yearly "annuity" payment, to be made each June, would therefore amount to as much as $150,000, an outlandish figure that the tribes more rationally thought of as twenty dollars per person.[9]

The U.S. government had in mind paying the Indians about ten cents per acre, and re-selling the same land to farmers for $1.50 per acre. The government profit on this transaction would easily cover the yearly annuity payment promised the Indians under the provisions of the Treaties.

The two treaties were concluded separately. The Treaty of Traverse des Sioux[10] was first, and was formally agreed to near St. Peter, Minnesota. The Territorial governor appointed by President Zachary Taylor, Alexander Ramsey, negotiated on behalf of the U.S. government. On a hilltop site chosen to encourage the wind to cool the participants— it was July—and beneath boughs of trees cut and fashioned to provide shade, the white men and the Indian chiefs made their deal.

Some of the Indians did not want to deal, but many more knew that the white men could not be stopped by their refusal to sell their land. The tribal leaders tried to hold out for a good price. The Treaty of Traverse des Sioux ceded the vast lands across southwestern Minnesota, and reserved for the Sisseton and Wahpeton Indians the ten miles either side of the Minnesota River between Lake Traverse and the mouth of the Yellow Medicine River. The Treaty of Mendota, concluded a bit later with the Mdewakanton and Wahpekute tribes further east, conceded similar lands in the southeastern portion of the Territory, reserving that same ten miles either side of the Minnesota between the Yellow Medicine and a point a little bit upstream of the town of Mankato, where the Minnesota River makes a sharp turn and begins flowing north.

It wasn't the first time the U.S. government and the Sioux leaders had used river geography to define their land deals. In 1805, President Jefferson sent U.S. Army Captain Zebulon Pike north on the Mississippi from St. Louis in search of a defensible outpost and the headwaters of the great river. Captain Pike and Mdewakanton Sioux leader Little Crow agreed to a deal over the lands nine miles either side of the Mississippi from roughly the mouth of the Minnesota to St. Anthony Falls. These lands would provide the government with the strategic bluffs used to build Fort Snelling, and with the larger area that would later become the cities of Minneapolis and St. Paul.[11]

Defining the Indian Reservation lands this way in 1851—ten miles either side of a roughly 100 mile stretch of the Minnesota River—was conveniently specific in such an undeveloped area. It was inconvenient for purposes of development, however. The Minnesota River was going to be the thoroughfare on which the bounty of the agricultural lands either side of it was going to pass—the railroad in the Midwest of the 1850s was largely an urban curiosity—and there couldn't have been a more certain way of causing friction between the Indians and the farmers.

The Minnesota River is a tremendous inland waterway that might be better known today but for a quirk of geologic history. Its last few miles as it approaches the Mississippi are low and flat, and it might have been considered the main channel of the great Mississippi. Had it been, the headwaters of the Mississippi would be quite different, for the simple reason that the Minnesota River can be followed all the way north to Hudson Bay and the Arctic Ocean. The Minnesota is traced upstream to two large, slender lakes that sit atop the Continental Divide—Big Stone Lake and Lake Traverse—that form part of the western edge of the state. The two lakes are connected by the Traverse Gap, a shallow little channel that can whimsically send water to either the Arctic Ocean via the Red River of the North or to the Gulf of Mexico and the Atlantic via the Minnesota and the Mississippi. President Jefferson's dream of an inland waterway across the Continent was realized in the Minnesota River—albeit in the wrong direction!

As befits a political occasion, solemn speeches were made at St. Peter that July in 1851 when the Treaty of Traverse des Sioux was concluded. The Indian chiefs made speeches. One of them, Chief Curly Head, made a speech that was perhaps as good and as prescient a speech as has ever been made by someone in his position. "Fathers," he said, "you think it is a great deal of money you are giving for this land. I do not think so, for both our lands and all the money we get for them will belong to the white man. The money comes to us but will all go to the white men who trade with us."[12]

By virtue of their treaty with the U.S. government, the Indians of southern Minnesota—people who had lived a hunter/gatherer life for centuries—were suddenly capitalists of a sort. They were capitalists, however, without the generations of fiscally circumspect forebears who could teach them the skills required to protect their capital from its natural predators.

The president of the Northwest Fur Company, future Minnesota Governor Henry Sibley, claimed he and his Northwest Fur Company were owed money for furs supposedly purchased from the Indians at inflated prices—lots of money, as it happens. He was given some $145,000

Henry H. Sibley, president of the Northwest Fir Company and the first governor of Minnesota.

out of the Treaty settlement for himself and his Company, a fortune in the 1850s, before the tribes saw a dime of the Treaty money.[13]

Agencies were set up along the Minnesota River to help organize the reservation and these new government lands, and—not incidentally—to facilitate trade with the Indians. In this second function, the system and human nature sowed the seeds of disaster. Chief Curly Head simply could not have been more far-sighted.

III

LOOKING ABOUT AT HIS four young children, Johan Kochendorfer of Woodford County, Illinois, must have had hopeful thoughts. He may have seen in his children future farm workers, eventually farm owners, the sort who might take over some of the day-to-day work from him, and then eventually the farm itself.

In September 1857, with most of the farming work done for the year, Johan and Catherine decided to try to strike out on their own with their growing family, leaving Catherine's sister and brother-in-law and their family behind in Illinois. The new lands that were just coming on the market for farming were north and west of them, in the Minnesota Territory, farmland thought to be less developed and, therefore, perhaps cheaper per acre than it was in central Illinois.

Travel across Illinois westward towards the Mississippi River was slow and difficult without rail lines, and rail lines were scarce in western Illinois in September 1857. The Kochendorfers traveled by covered wagon, all their worldly possessions in satchels and bags. Little Margaret was still less than a year old—she would cut three teeth during the journey—a precious additional bit of cargo. Wagon travel was slow and jarring, and in the lower spots of the road, the wagon wheels would have pelted them with mud. The Kochendorfers and their wagon would pull up to farm houses and ask to spend the night inside or alongside the barn. It is hard for us today to fully grasp how difficult travel across land was before the railroad and the automobile: it was tedious, slow, and for us moderns, almost unimaginably difficult.

They met other German-speaking people as they made their way north and west through Illinois, to the Mississippi River, and they were told the Minnesota Territory was being overrun with grasshoppers, that the price of food was consequently very high, and that the people there were starving. What a dreadful thing if it were true! How could one know for sure? One couldn't. That was the difficult thing. Johan and Catherine decided to forge on anyway.

The Kochendorfers appear to have gone north, along the Illinois River, to the town of Peru. They then crossed the river and struck out overland, to the northwest, towards the Mississippi. The flat Illinois plain ends and it begins to get hilly as the traveler approaches Wisconsin, and Catherine later described that near Mount Carroll "we encountered the worst roads—up one hill and down another." They reached the Mississippi at what was then called Dunleith, and what is today East Dubuque, Illinois.

By this time they were tired, and they noticed the hay they were buying to feed the horses "that in the beginning of the trip had cost five or ten cents cost twenty five or fifty," Catherine would write later in describing the trip, "and we were afraid as it was getting cooler and the weather was so changeable that we now decided to take the steamboat to St. Paul."

Passage up the Mississippi by steamboat was much easier, and the Kochendorfers landed in St. Paul in early fall. They found lodgings easily enough, and the grasshoppers were nowhere in sight. They had almost no money left, so they were gratified to learn that prices weren't nearly as high as they had been told.

Catherine had promised her sister Rosina in Illinois a letter, but the hustle and activity involved in learning the ways of a new town kept her very busy. St. Paul was a bustling pioneer town of 10,000 or so in 1857, the largest town she had ever lived in, and she had to learn how to get by with very little English. It could not have been easy. She found a church for them all to attend, and although the services were conducted in German, they were different and at first it was all unfamiliar.

It was not until early November before she was able to sit down and write. Pen in hand, she could not help but reflect on how far she had come, how she was now separated completely from the Lechler family, even from her beloved sister Rosina, for the first time in her life.

The trip and the new circumstances were all very interesting, however, and she must have been almost overflowing with thoughts and emotions as she filled the lined, light slate-gray pages with her neat, thin, very vertical German script, knowing that she could tell her sister so far away of all that she had seen. This letter, carefully preserved by sister Rosina and then later by other family members—the ink quite faded now—survives today:

St. Paul, Minn. Territory, Nov.2, 1857
Dearly Beloved Sister and Brother-in-Law,
May the Grace of our Lord and Savior Jesus Christ, the love of God, and the Communion of His Soul be with you all. Amen.
I feel so happy, and thankful to God, that His wisdom so arranged it, that although we are separated, we may, with pen, ink, and paper have heartfelt talks, which is especially very dear

to me at this time. I assure you that I miss you so much. Many, many times I wish I could be in your midst, though I have not regretted our coming here, but love draws me to you—but I am living in hopes. Dear Sister, I promised you that within one month of our departure you should have a letter, but it will not be quite as soon as that, for unavoidable reasons.

Catherine discusses the journey, mentions the expenses incurred, and then comments that the boat fare to St. Paul came to twenty-five dollars. She then discussed their living arrangements:

We rented a cabin—about 13 by 19 feet in size—but now it is well and nicely furnished on the inside. We pay four dollars a month for it. We put a barn up for the horses which is to come out of our rent, as our landlord will keep it. (They live on the same lot with us. They are Catholics.)

Business here is quite dull. A man, with his team, gets five dollars a day. According to that we can easily make a living this winter, if Johan gets enough work to keep busy.

Dear Sister, you have no cause to worry about us, even if our money is almost used up . . .

Catherine's concern for horses and barns and business is a concern for Johan's work. Johan would work in St. Paul at what was called "drayage," a now largely defunct word meaning that Johan used a team of horses, "dray horses," to move goods, work that today is done through the moving/storage and trucking trade. The trick in making a living at drayage was to feed and maintain a good team of horses and to keep them busy enough to earn more than that required to feed them.

As might be gleaned from the passage from the Apostle Paul's letters that Catherine used to start her own letter, she wanted to discuss with her sister their religious life in this town named for that very same Saint Paul:

We live quite close to our little church. It is quite pretty and comfortable. It was built this past summer, but alas, there is but a very small congregation. There are not many members here. We enjoy the services . . . still we do not feel quite at home among them yet. The singing is still strange to us, and our love for you, our dear brothers and sisters, makes us think back and prompts us to often pray for you.

Catherine is referring to the Evangelical Association church that was constructed on the corner of Eleventh and Pine streets, an intersection that in 1857 was on the northeast outskirts of the city. Catherine would remedy the situation of not feeling quite at home in this particular congregation. A few months later, the Kochendorfers became one of the founding families of *die Kirche der Dreieinigkeit Evangelisch Lutherisch*, or the Trinity Evangelical Church (later Salem Evangelical Church).[14] Apart from the Kochendorfers, there are only ten families listed in the initial 1858 rolls. One of them—a Mr. and Mrs. Gottfried Schmidt, a nearby farming family—would become very, very important to the Kochendorfers in the years to come.

Six-year-old Johan evidently had a broken arm that was bandaged throughout the journey from Illinois:

> When we took the bandages off his broken arm, we found it had not been properly set, so it was crooked, but he has no pain and we are in hopes that he will not be inconvenienced with it. He asks me to tell you about it. Rosina also asks me to tell her godmother and godfather that they should come here. [Daughter] Catherine says she will cook apples, dumplings, potatoes and cabbage for you when you come.

Catherine concludes her letter to her beloved sister as follows:

> Now Rose, please write real soon to us. I should love to have a letter right now. How is your little Mary? And the other children? Remember us to all the brothers and sisters in the congregation and the Blue Creek congregation [in Illinois], and also father and mother. In closing, I wish you God's rich blessing, peace and unity and we ask for your believing prayers on our behalf. May God's Grace lead and guide us, so we may be true and faithful to the end, is the prayer of your loving sister,
> Catherine Lechler Kochendorfer

Catherine's letter was long, but she graciously gave her husband a little space towards the end. Johan concludes matters as follows:

> The peace of God be with you. Amen. Because Catherine has written quite a lengthy letter I will be brief. You know likely that I do not like to write. I want you to know how it is about getting land here. Around St. Paul it is quite hilly. It is also uneven and sandy, but very fertile. Everything grows well, especially potatoes. We bought some potatoes from a German man, who had three acres in potatoes, from which he harvested 600 bushels. He sold them at 50 cents per bushel, and received $300.00. He paid $10 rent per acre per year. He lives about five miles from here.
>
> Land is very expensive around St. Paul. Another man purchased forty acres, two miles out for $500 and there was a frame house on this land. Ten acres are under cultivation and the rest is not cleared. By this you can judge what a poor man can do here, but you must not be discouraged, for there are many other opportunities also.
>
> Last week I drove ninety miles up the Minnesota River which runs somewhat south from here to a new little town named Mankato. There are still good opportunities there. People there told me that 15 miles farther on there was fine land to be opened next spring which they report is very good land.
>
> I did not see this land. When I left home last week I expected to take a claim while up there. When I arrived I learned that you must be on it thirty days before applying for it and that was too long for me to stay and too expensive also . . .

The Kochendorfers had only been in St. Paul a month or so when they set these words to paper, but already one can see Johan and Catherine's plans developing. Land is expensive in and around St. Paul, but Johan already knows of the good land becoming available along the Minnesota River south of St. Paul, near Mankato.

Johan closes the letter by confessing to his in-laws in Illinois his plan: He would make the trek back to Mankato the following

March, this time prepared with the time and money to stake a claim to some of this rich farmland alongside the Minnesota, upstream from Mankato, perhaps near the land the Sioux Indians had reserved for themselves under the Treaties of 1851. Johan may have had in mind farming land that was just outside the Sioux land, either close to Mankato or more than ten miles from the Minnesota River.

Johan did not make this trek in March 1858. The exact reasons are unclear. Perhaps the winter had yet to break up—could the Kochendorfers have even believed that winters in St. Paul could be still longer and deeper than those in central Illinois?—or perhaps his business did not allow him to accumulate the needed money. Whatever the case, we know that he did not stake his claim in 1858.

We do know that his dream to do so did not die that winter. Four years later he would realize that dream of farming the rich soil alongside the Minnesota River, just upstream from Mankato.

IV

THE KOCHENDORFERS WERE NOT the only ones dreaming of this land alongside the Minnesota River in November 1857. The U.S. government had big plans for that land as well.

It was May of the following year that Minnesota was officially admitted as the thirty-second state of the Union. St. Paul was named the capital city. Henry Sibley was elected governor. Sibley was a trader, a man in the classic tradition of the frontiersman. He saw statehood as primarily a form of commercial progress, and he couldn't help looking upon the bustle of the capital city of St. Paul with pride when he remembered what a primitive outpost it had been only a few years before.

It had only been a dozen years earlier that the landing area that became St. Paul was known as Pig's Eye, after the local moonshiner Pierre "Pig's Eye" Parrant, a somewhat disreputable character with one bad eye and a squint, a man who lived and worked a fair fraction of his life in the caves that formed easily in the limestone cliffs alongside the Mississippi.[15]

The first church near the landing was called St. Paul's, and a few years later the city leaders decided a proper name was needed. A poem appeared in The St. Paul Press newspaper in 1851, having some fun with this civic metamorphosis:

> Pig's Eye, converted thou shalt be, like Saul;
> Arise, and be, henceforth, St. Paul![16]

Henry Sibley understood the state's potential for monetary abundance as few others could, and he knew the only way to take full commercial advantage of it was to control the Indian population. He pushed the U.S. government to modify the terms of the Treaties of 1851.

Weeks after granting statehood to Minnesota, the U.S. government convened another treaty conference with the Sioux, this time in Washington, D.C., to modify the terms of the Treaties of Mendota and Traverse des Sioux. Nine Indian chiefs made the long trek to Washington to negotiate and then sign the new treaty, which effectively shrunk the Indian lands again in return for still more money.[17] The tribes relinquished the land north and east of the Minnesota River, leaving them only the land south and west of the River, extending back—as before—ten miles from the river's edge.

The tribal leaders involved must have had a rough time of it that year. Their travel to Washington must have been eye-opening: the huge masses of white men living so vigorously and inexplicably along the eastern coast, the power of the railroad lines that could trample anything in their path, the pomp and majesty of the capital city. Then, later that same year, the difficult task of explaining to their fellow tribesmen the loss of the land on the northeast side of the river in return for more of these nebulous monetary promises. Most difficult of all, perhaps, was trying to explain to their fellow tribesmen the magnitude of this force arrayed against them and their way of life. We can't know how hard they tried to communicate this last harsh truth, but their unquestioned leadership of their tribes was never the same.

The Mdewakanton Sioux leader sent from the lower Minnesota River valley tribe was Little Crow, grandson of the Chief Little Crow who had negotiated with U.S. Army Captain Zebulon Pike in 1805 over the lands either side of the Mississippi.

Little Crow's family had had dealings with now Governor Henry Sibley and the Northwest Fur Company going back to the 1830s. Sibley went on months-long winter hunts with Little Crow and his tribe when they stayed the winter on their Kaposia grounds near St. Paul. Sibley's interest in doing so was commercial, because he sought to enlist the Indians in his fur trading operation. Early twentieth-century Minnesota historian Solon Buck described the operation: "The trader had furnished [the Indian] with guns, blankets, and powder and shot on credit in the fall," a transaction that would be easier to put over if the Indian had seen the accuracy and power of these guns in action in Sibley's own hands. "When the winter was over . . . [the Indian hunter] gave enough furs to the trader to pay his debt, and then if he had any furs left he bought what he pleased with them."[18]

This last bit of business the two parties did together was interesting. "The Indians bought many trinkets, and paid good prices for them," Buck continued. "Looking-glasses costing four cents in St. Louis were sold to the Indians for four muskrat furs, or the value of eighty cents. A pound of tobacco costing the trader twelve cents was sold for eight skins, or $1.60."[19]

After the trader bought the furs, he turned them over to Sibley in Mendota, near St. Paul. Sibley shipped them off to Mackinac on Lake Huron, headquarters of the American Fur Company, and from there these furs went around the world: New York, London, mainland Europe, even to China. Sibley was becoming a wealthy man, in part due to his good relations with Little Crow and his tribe.

Little Crow thought of himself as the unquestioned leader of his people, and this sense of noblesse oblige he carried with him to Washington, D.C. He affected civilized manners and dress in dealing with the government in Washington, wearing black formal clothing and velvet collars when meeting with President Buchanan.[20]

Little Crow could see with his own eyes that this powerful new force on the continent was not one that could be stopped, and he, therefore, decided to make what he could of a hopeless bargaining position. His people back on the reservation would simply have to understand that he was looking after their interests, and this was the best deal they could expect.

It is only natural that many members of his tribe, members who had never traveled east and seen this new, powerful presence, would wonder whether Little Crow truly had their interests first in his mind.

AT ABOUT THIS SAME TIME, Johan and Catherine got themselves and their children into their Sunday best and made their way to a photography studio to have a family picture taken. That photograph survives today. Johan is stiff and clean shaven and rigid and looks uncomfortable in his black suit. His wife, Catherine, sits alongside him and looks serenely at the camera. Johan, Jr., stands in back, a confused and uncertain seven-year-old, his hair hastily matted down. Rosina stands alongside her father and looks somewhat sternly at the camera. Margaret and Catherine sit in their parents' laps and lean back against them, uncertain of the meaning of the camera and the cameraman and clearly preferring to remain in their parents' arms.

Also around this same time, Johan's interest in farming and new farming techniques got him to invest in and become part owner of a threshing machine. His was the first of its kind in the area. These large machines separated wheat from the stalks and husks using a rotating mechanical separator. Johan used his horses, harnessed to the machine and walking in circles, to generate the rotational power for his threshing machine. The machine was normally placed high up on wheels and could thereby move about the wheat field, in this way going where the harvesting needed to be done. His machine would be hired by nearby farmers at harvest time to avoid the tedious work of manually separating the wheat kernels from the plants.

The Kochendorfers welcomed yet another child into their family in the spring of 1859. She was called Sarah, a somewhat less Germanic name that perhaps signaled the family's growing comfort with the language being spoken all around them, the language of the majority of the citizens of St. Paul. Johan and Catherine and their children were daily becoming more comfortable with the ways of their new, adopted country.

V

THE COUNTRY WAS BECOMING increasingly uncomfortable, however. The issue of slavery dominated national politics as the citizens of Minnesota readied to vote for president for the first time in 1860, and the political lines were sharply drawn.

The precise legal issue at the center of the 1860 campaign was whether the federal government had the power to simply prevent the spread of slavery into the new western territories like Minnesota. Stephen Douglas, the Illinois senator, was the Democratic Party candidate for president, and he believed the federal government had no such power.

Douglas argued that the Constitution did not reserve for the federal government this power to prevent new states from deciding on their own as to whether to enforce slave contracts. It was a "state's rights" issue, Douglas argued, and he used the Tenth Amendment to the U.S. Constitution to reason that all powers not specifically given to the federal government by the Constitution were state powers, and, therefore, individual states should be able to decide for themselves whether to adopt slavery.[21] It is an argument whose logical framework is used today in addressing very different issues.

Abraham Lincoln of Springfield was familiar with the Douglas argument. In fact, Lincoln had debated Douglas seven times in 1858 throughout the state when the two of them were campaigning for a U.S. Senate appointment. Lincoln had even edited and then published the texts of those debates. The published work showed Lincoln's skill in debating Douglas, and Lincoln was gradually gaining admirers throughout the country.

Lincoln was a prominent member of the western contingent of the new anti-slavery Republican Party, but the eastern members of the Republican Party hadn't heard him, and he was invited to New York to address the Young Men's Republican Union to make his case. He worked for months on his argument, researching and refining points he had made to Douglas in person eighteen months before.[22] When the time came, he struggled to his feet—"He was tall, tall, oh how tall" wrote one observer, "and so angular and awkward that I had, for an instant, a feeling of pity for so ungainly a man"[23]—in the Great Hall in beautiful Cooper Union in New York City on February 27, 1860. This angular and awkward man then commenced to cut the Douglas argument to shreds.

Lincoln started off by quoting Douglas from the *New York Times*: "Our fathers, when they framed the Government under which we live, understood this question just as well, and even better, than we do now."

Mr. Lincoln endorsed this view, and allowed this endorsement to focus the issue. "Let us now inquire whether the 'thirty-nine,' or any of them," Lincoln continued, referring to the thirty-nine framers of the Constitution, "ever acted upon this question; and if they did, how they acted upon it—how they expressed that better understanding?"

Lincoln proceeded to trace the voting histories of each of the framers back to points in their political careers when they may have been asked to vote on this very issue—for example, when, in 1784, the Congress of the Confederation voted on whether to permit slavery in the Northwestern Territories, the area north and west of the Ohio and east of the Mississippi. He showed that as members of the Federal Congress or the Congress of the Confederation, twenty-one of these thirty-nine framers had no trouble finding that the federal government had such power to prevent slavery in new federal territory, while only a few voted to extend slavery to these territories. (Lincoln also made the legal point that a federal legislator could vote to extend slavery without reaching the question as to whether the federal government had the power to prevent such extension, but such a person could not vote to prevent extension without believing the federal government had the power to do so.) Lincoln went on to observe that some of the others who had not been federal legislators and, therefore, hadn't voted squarely on the issue were well known for their anti-slavery sentiments, men such as Benjamin Franklin and Alexander Hamilton. A clear majority of the framers, therefore, believed the federal government had the power to prevent the extension of slavery to new territories.

Abraham Lincoln at Cooper Union, February 1860.

Lincoln urged, then, that the federal government exercise this power. "If our sense of duty forbids this [i.e., the spread of slavery], then let us stand by our duty," he argued, before concluding: "Let us have faith that Right makes Might, in that faith, let us, to the end, dare to do our duty as we understand it."

This was no idle dare to duty, of course. War was potentially in the balance.

Many of the easterners entering Cooper Union that evening had assumed this painfully thin, awkward fellow from the backwoods was out of his league as a national leader. By the time they left that night, the opinion of many of them had changed. "No man ever before made such an impression on his first appeal to a New York audience,"[24] gushed one reporter. Copies of the speech were widely circulated, and Lincoln's centrist position—limiting slavery to where it existed rather than either ignoring or abolishing it—gained adherents. It was the evening when Abraham Lincoln became the intellectual leader of the Republican Party.

MINNESOTANS KNEW WHICH SIDE of this legal issue they were on. Historian Solon Buck wrote in the 1920s of his fellow Minnesotans that "the German and Scandinavian immigrants all looked with horror on negro slavery."[25] Perhaps some Minnesotans also resented the southern notion that farming work was so menial as to be the work of slaves. Whatever the reason, Minnesotans were with the Republicans—most of them—through and through.

When the Republican Party nominated this simple yet eloquent lawyer from central Illinois—that same lawyer who had agreed to defend Mrs. Melissa Goings back in 1857 in Woodford County—Minnesotans gave him 63.4 percent of their votes, an amazing majority in an election with four candidates.

The election of Abraham Lincoln in November 1860 was a watershed event. The southern states knew that there was no longer room for a compromise on the issue of slavery, at least not one that they could find acceptable. They formed a confederacy, and their army attacked the U.S. Army outpost at Fort Sumter in South Carolina the following April, and the most cataclysmic event in American history began.

Notes

[1] Much of this land is today part of the country of Moldova.

[2] It's roughly 1,000 miles from southern Germany to Bessarabia, but the two regions are connected by the Danube River.

[3] *From Catherine to Khruschev—The Story of Russia's Germans* by Giesinger (1974). The official term used to describe the expulsion was "resettlement," and it was technically voluntary.

[4] *Justice Served: Abraham Lincoln and the Melissa Goings Case* by J. Myers (2007).

[5] E.g., Founding Fathers Thomas Jefferson and James Madison were Virginians who did not agree very often with or even trust Alexander Hamilton of New York or John Adams of Massachusetts, and the feeling was mutual.

[6] The many Indian tribes that lived in the area extending west from the Mississippi to the Missouri River and as far west as present-day Montana were united by a common language, and they called themselves "Dakotah," or "Lakota." "Sioux" is a name given them by others. However, the Mdewakanton tribe of Dakotah, who lived throughout southern Minnesota and who are central to this story, now refer to themselves as "Mdewakanton Sioux." Much of the early writing done by the white settlers refer to them as "Sioux," and to prevent confusion this word will sometimes be used. No offense is intended.

[7] *Light and Shadows of a Long Episcopate* by Bishop H.B. Whipple (1899), Chapter X.

[8] Ibid.

[9] *The Great Sioux Uprising* by C.M. Oehler (1959), p. 12-14.

[10] "Traverse des Sioux" refers to a point on the Minnesota River near St. Peter where crossing the river is easy and safe most of the time.

[11] *Stories of Early Minnesota* by Solon and Elizabeth Buck (1926), p. 85. Solon Buck was a professor of history at the University of Minnesota and superintendent of the Minnesota Historical Society, and later archivist of the United States.

[12] Buck, p. 177.

[13] Oehler, p. 14.

[14] The small white chapel built by this small congregation in 1874 is now known as "Old Salem Church," and is located on Upper Fifty-Fifth Street in Inver Grove Heights, along the south shore of Schmidt Lake. A plaque out front lists the family names of those early members.

[15] *St. Paul—The First 150 Years* by V. Kunz (1991), p. 11.

[16] Buck, p. 165.

[17] Oehler, p. 14.

[18] Buck, p. 132.

[19] Ibid.

[20] *Lincoln and the Sioux Uprising of 1862* by Hank H. Cox (2005), p. 22

[21] Senator Douglas, at Alton, Illinois on October 15th, 1858 put it this way in his debate with Lincoln: "We ought to extend to the negro race all the rights, all the privileges, and all the immunities which they can exercise consistently with the safety of society. Humanity requires that we should give them all these privileges; Christianity commands that we should extend those privileges to them. The question then arises, 'What are those privileges, and what is the nature and extent of them?' My answer is, that is a question which each State must answer for itself."

[22] *Herndon's Lincoln* by W. Herndon (1889), Volume III, p. 454: "Meanwhile he [Lincoln] spent the intervening time in careful preparation. He searched through the dusty volumes of congressional proceedings in the State library, and dug deeply into political history. He was painstaking and thorough in the study of his subject, but when at last he left for New York we had many misgivings—and he not a few himself—of his success in the great metropolis."

[23] *New York Tribune*, February 28, 1860.

[24] *Abraham Lincoln: The Prairie and the War Years* by C. Sandburg, p. 165.

[25] Buck, p. 195.

The Republican Party Platform of 1860, a blazing fireball of change.

"And the War Came"

ABRAHAM LINCOLN and the Republicans of 1860 had run on a platform that not only opposed the spread of slavery, but also declared that secession from the Union—"disunion"—was illegal and would be considered a treasonous act. It didn't take long for some of the southern states to test the resolve of the new Lincoln administration on this second point: South Carolina seceded on December 20th, and six other states joined them even before Lincoln took the oath of office on March 4th, 1861. In fact, a Confederate Congress comprising representatives of these seceding states was convened in Montgomery, Alabama, and Jefferson Davis was elected its president and inaugurated before Abraham Lincoln took his oath.

Lincoln and the Republicans were forced to treat the secession of these states as treason. Yet Lincoln hoped to avoid the use of arms to resolve the issue. The attack on Fort Sumter changed all that, and indicated that the South was fully prepared to fight to defend its right to secede.

The early skirmishes of the Civil War were filled with uncertainty as to the rules of engagement and the depth of each side's commitment. The generals of both the North and South knew one another personally—many had gone to West Point Academy together—and they seemed to be trying their best to avoid too much bloodshed. They seemed to be hoping against hope that the politicians would figure a way out of the mess and keep them from engaging in what must have appeared to them to be fratricide.

The fighting, once started, would snowball in intensity. By mid-year 1862, enough blood had been spilled that the two sides hated one another, and they then understood it to be a fight to the end.

The fighting that had been going on in Congress for years would now move to the battlefield. Congress had been a bitter, acrimonious place for many years prior to the outbreak of hostilities, but when the southerners left town a common purpose was easy to develop among the remaining members in Washington, D.C.

One result of this new-found consensus was the Homestead Act of 1862. Versions of such an act had kicked around Congress for many years, but the southern delegations were opposed because they believed it would favor the growth and power of the northern states. One such act passed the House in 1858 but was defeated by one vote in the Senate. In 1860, both houses passed their own versions, and a final version survived a contentious conference committee fight on June 19th, but President Buchanan did not want to offend southern interests, and he hastily vetoed the bill on the 22nd.

The limiting of slavery and the idea of a Homestead Act had very similar political implications. If slavery could be prevented in the new territories by Lincoln and the Republicans, the influence of southern slave interests would necessarily dwindle in Washington, D.C., with their diminishing voting percentages. Likewise, a Homestead Act would encourage development of the agricultural lands of the Upper Mississippi and Missouri River valleys, and these new free-states full of homesteaders would gain political influence at the expense of the South. Southerners were fighting a battle on both fronts to hold onto their power in Washington, D.C.

LINCOLN AND THE REPUBLICANS of 1860 made both limiting the spread of slavery as well as advocating homestead legislation, specifically "free homestead" legislation, central planks in their party platform.

Lincoln and the Republicans of 1860 were revolutionaries of a sort we have trouble seeing clearly today, both because of the Civil War and because the material progress they championed triumphed so completely. They were men of a miraculous time and place to such an extent that many of the ideas and policies they advocated in 1860 would have been unthinkable only fifty years before, and would be taken for granted fifty years later.

The year 1860 was the mid-point of a century of such technical progress that it was suddenly possible to think in startlingly new ways about the economic prospects of each citizen, and it was the Republicans of 1860 who were doing this sort of thinking. They advocated the building of the transcontinental railroad, and saw it through to completion in 1869. Lincoln understood the collective effort a railroad future required—he had been a lawyer for the Illinois Central—and he saw the need on occasion for stepping on a few individual property rights in return for a larger, more valuable railroad property that could benefit all.

Reflect a minute on the world Lincoln was born into in 1809, and contrast it with the world he saw coming into being in the late 1850s. In 1809, electricity was only observed—it was not generated and transmitted at will by people. The railroad, indeed the steam engine, was largely unknown. Long-distance communication was done strictly by letter carried by wagon or horseback.

By 1860, electricity had been harnessed and bent to useful ends, and most of the laws of electro-magnetism were being formulated. Steamboat service became important in the 1820s, and by 1860 it had completely revolutionized river travel. Thomas Jefferson had died only thirty-four years before, but he never saw a railroad line or a train. By 1860, the railroad was not only being developed—it was becoming commonplace in and between large cities, and it was making Mr. Lincoln a wealthy man. No photographs of Jefferson were ever taken, while thousands of photographs were taken of Lincoln and his contemporaries. Morse Code had been developed in the 1830s, and by 1860 communication along the many new telegraph lines was instantaneous. It was enough to make a person's head spin! Lincoln had been a seventeen-year-old when Thomas Jefferson had gone to his deathbed having lived a life materially similar to that of Cicero or Plato: parchment, horses, swords, slaves. As a man in his forties and fifties, Abraham Lincoln was living a life that, in certain material respects, Jefferson would hardly recognize.

Read in its entirety, the Republican Party and their platform of 1860 is a blazing fireball of change to the world and the order and the limits placed upon humans since Ancient Rome. The 1860 Republicans envisioned a future in which people would no longer require teams of horses—fed and cared for by armies of serfs—to transport them about the town and the county. Republicans planned for an "iron horse" to spirit the citizenry across the entire continent! No longer would citizens require dozens of field hands to gather the foods that the few living the "good life" required. The growing productivity of individual farmers and their excess production would provide all that was required, and this excess food would be shuttled to the cities and wherever it was wanted by steam-boats and the new railroad lines. By simple process of logic, then, no more would legions of men have to be born into a life of servitude to sustain the easy lives of the well-born. Republicans were the anti-slavery party right down to their very boot bottoms: on moral grounds certainly, but also because slavery and serfdom in general were to be thrown out along with all the other unnecessary, dust-covered impedimenta of antiquity!

For evidence of the effect this seemingly boundless material progress had on this new Republican Party, consider declaration #3 of the Republican Party Platform agreed upon in Chicago in May of 1860, in which the party sets out the reasoning behind its firm stance against secession. "That to the Union of the States, this nation owes its unprecedented increase of population," they crowed, "its surprising development of material resources, its rapid augmentation of wealth, its happiness at home and its honor abroad; and we hold in abhor-rence all schemes for disunion."

For these Republicans of 1860, then, secession, or "disunion," was treason not merely as a legal or moral matter, but because the Union was such a complete and unalloyed economic and political success!

The Republican Party position on halting the spread of slavery was spelled out further down, in declarations #7 through #9, its position on homestead legislation in declaration #13, its "railroad to the Pacific"—with mail delivery!—in declaration #16, but these declarations were all of a piece, and that larger whole was growth, and wealth, and progress for all.

In its various incarnations, the idea of a Homestead Act was to put federal lands in private hands for agricultural development, and the political question was how this should be brought about, and how easy the terms would be for the homesteader. For the reasons mentioned, it was the northern states that saw this as a boon: they had plenty of rich farmland that was still federal property, and plenty of ambitious citizens ready to pull up stakes and go farm it.

The Kochendorfers of St. Paul were precisely the sort of people that the northern states saw as the beneficiaries of such an act, and precisely the sort of people the Republicans of 1860 wanted to help.

With the onset of hostilities in 1861 and the disappearance of the southern congressional delegations from Washington, D.C., the barriers that would otherwise have moderated the provisions of the resulting Homestead Act were removed. The northern states could now put together all the generous provisions that had previously been politically unworkable. The resulting Homestead Act of 1862 passed in a landslide: the House of Representatives passed this new act easily in February 1862 by a vote of 107 to 16. The Senate passed it in May by a vote of 33 to 7.

The Homestead Act was signed into law by President Lincoln on May 20, 1862. Lincoln didn't comment much on the Act's passage, perhaps reasoning that speeches are mere self-congratulation at that point, and perhaps realizing his enemies would undoubtedly get themselves all worked up and criticize whatever he said in its defense.

The provisions of the Act were well known for weeks beforehand. The act stipulated that the head of a family could lay claim to 160 acres of federal land, and by improving that land and farming it for five years, this "homesteader" could pay a small registration fee and claim clear title to that land. (If willing to pay $1.25 per acre, or $200, the homesteader could acquire the clear title to those 160 acres in six months.)

For good measure, the 1862 Congress added a feature to the Act that the Republicans of 1860 could never have fully envisioned. The Homestead Act of 1862, signed by President Lincoln, also stipulated that eligible homesteaders could "never have borne arms against the U.S. Government," effectively making all members of the Confederate war effort ineligible for the benefits of the act. There was a war on, after all!

II

THE DIARIES OF MERIWETHER LEWIS and William Clark are quite detailed in their observations of the Native Americans they encountered in 1804 and 1805 as their Corps of Discovery made its trailblazing expedition to the Pacific, including some of the many Sioux tribes. Lewis was moved to observe that among "all the Indians of America, bravery is esteemed the primary virtue, nor can anyone become eminent among them who has not at some period of his life given proof of possessing this virtue. With them there can be no preferment without some warlike achievement."[1]

Their Enlightenment sensibilities led Lewis and Clark to encourage the Indians to strive to live in peace and harmony, not only with white men but with the other tribes of Indians. It was not an easy sell. Lewis records that after one such effort at counseling peace and harmony, one young warrior asked "what the nation would do for Chiefs?"[2] Chiefs were critical to tribal organization, and chiefs were often chosen by their leadership and accomplishments in battle.

The Lewis and Clark view of Indian culture was heavily influenced by the fact that they dealt almost exclusively with tribal leaders, for whom such warlike achievements were central to their role as chiefs. There were other aspects of Indian culture and character that Lewis and Clark, and later the government they represented, did not see or fully appreciate. They saw these qualities in the calmness and patience and honesty and wisdom of their Indian guides—Sacagawea, a Shoshone, and George Drouillard, whose mother was a Shawnee. Their writings, however, suggest they regarded these good qualities as particular to their fellow Corps of Discovery members, and not general Indian characteristics. It was a mistake of reasoning that would be made many more times by many others.

The Treaties of 1851 and 1858 had not immediately altered much the life of the Indians of southern Minnesota. They still hunted and camped about the lands they had sold to the U.S. government, and in those early years they must have regarded the treaty provisions as somewhat quaint legalistic nonsense. The yearly annuity payments were often much smaller than the amounts stipulated due to the borrowings the Indians made from the agencies, but the Indians had no use for the money as such, so as long as the agents were willing to advance more food and clothing against next year's payment the arrangement seemed to work.

The treaties had undermined tribal organization, however. The chiefs were seen by their fellow tribesmen to be conceding land without a fight, and, therefore, not at all the battle leaders they were supposed to be. Without such battles, it was simply unclear who the true tribal chiefs were, and how the tribes would organize themselves.

Episcopalian Bishop Henry Whipple was sent to Minnesota to head up the diocese in the late 1850s. He saw the Indians as part of his diocese, and he befriended and hoped to convert them, and in doing this he became a student of their culture and their organization. He was a skilled political observer, and he could see potential political problems with the government's treatment of the Indians as sovereign nations, and he commented on this in his writings. "In all our relations with the Indians we have persistently carried out the idea that they were a sovereign people," he wrote in the 1860s. "If it is true that a nation cannot exist within a nation, that these heathen were to send no ambassadors to us and we none to them, that they had no power to compel us to observe it for themselves, then our first step was a fatal step. They did not possess a single element of sovereignty; and had they possessed it, we could not, in justice to ourselves, have permitted them to exercise it in the duties necessary to a nation's self-existence."[3]

Bishop Whipple then went on to observe that the entire idea of a treaty with these Indians undermined the tribal authority that would allow the treaty to work. "Because we had treated with them as an independent nation, we left them without government. Their own rude patriarchal government was always weakened and often destroyed by the new treaty relations. The chiefs lost all independence of action, and sooner or later became the pliant tools of traders and agents, powerful for mischief, but powerless for good. Nothing was given to supply the place of this defective tribal government."[4]

Thus, Lincoln's "men of progress" needed to deal with and make treaties with the Indian tribal leaders in order to extend their material plans. The treaty itself, however, undermined the authority of the Indian leaders, and in doing so undermined the enforcement of its terms.

A very practical example of this lack of true Indian government was the tribe's inability to punish wrong-doers. Murder was not uncommon, much of it between members of the same tribe, but the tribes had no good way to punish such behavior or to protect the tribe. Violent or obnoxious members were often cast out from the main settlements, but this involved no confinement, no permanent banishment.

Bishop Whipple wrote to President Lincoln in March 1862 about this lack of any enforceable criminal law within the tribes, paying particular attention to the effect this had on the law-abiding Indian. "The United States has virtually left the Indian without protection," he wrote Lincoln, identifying with and emphasizing the plight of the peaceful, law-abiding Indian citizen living in such a lawless area, and Lincoln's governmental responsibility. "I can count up more than a dozen murders which have taken place in the Chippewa County within two years . . . There is no law to protect the innocent or punish the guilty."[5]

Lawlessness might be restrained by strong tribal leadership, of course, but the power of the chiefs was undermined by a reservation system that eroded the source of the chief's power to impose tribal discipline—organizing the defense of their lands. Those who might be cast out of the main settlement for violent or other bad behavior knew that in the event the tribe was threatened, they would be called back and charged with attacking or defending against the enemy.

An example of such an individual was a Mdewakanton Sioux warrior in Little Crow's tribe named Mah-pa-o-ke-ne-jin ("Who Stands on a Cloud"), but the whites knew him as Cut-Nose, a name that referred to a gash thought to have been acquired—fittingly enough—in a fight with another warrior tribesman, John Otherday.[6] Cut-Nose was given to fighting, and to riling many of his fellow tribesmen: he was openly promiscuous with women belonging to others[7] and inclined to drink.[8] He may have blamed the white men for selling him the liquor that would cause his bad behavior. He was a proud warrior, though, and would have viewed with disapproval the adoption of the white men's ways among his fellow tribesmen, which might explain his fight with John Otherday, a strong warrior who had gladly taken up farming on the reservation lands in a very public way.

Mah-pa-o-ke ne-jin, "Cut Nose."

Another cast-off from a Lower Sioux tribe was a fellow named Red Middle Voice, or "Hochokaduta" or "Ho-choke-pe-doota." He was part of Chief Shakopee's tribe—in fact, the chief was actually Red Middle Voice's nephew. Red Middle Voice and his group were "discontented spirits . . . who had left their bands because of quarrels, strifes, or feuds."[9] They lived—some fifty of them—a few miles further upstream from Chief Shakopee's tribe, near where Rice Creek flows into the Minnesota River from the west. Outposts such as this one along Rice Creek were sometimes called a "Soldiers' Lodge," a term that conveyed the sense they were warriors and not interested in adopting the white man's ways—and that they were independent of the chiefs.[10] He and his group were regarded by the other Lower Sioux as "troublemakers" and "malcontents,"[11] and Red Middle Voice himself as "little better than an outlaw."[12]

Chief Little Crow and Chief Shakopee had no way to sanction Cut-Nose or Red Middle Voice. They had no prisons, no effective method of protecting their fellow tribesmen or their women from them. Equally troubling, Cut-Nose and Red Middle Voice knew that if they were to lose favor with the tribe and be banished, they would still be welcomed back in the event of a war against the Chippewa or any other tribe or nation.

III

JOHAN KOCHENDORFER OF ST. PAUL knew this was his time. It was early 1862, and events were falling in line to make his dreams of returning to a farming life possible. The Homestead Act would be passed by Congress, which meant land he had always had in mind to farm, the miraculously rich land along the Minnesota River upstream from Mankato, would become free to whoever wanted to go and improve it. He could also be sure others had similar plans, other ambitious farmers anxious to "preempt" the act and begin fencing off and improving 160 acres of that beautiful black soil. How could he not feel the time was now?

Catherine must have had a few misgivings. She had four young daughters under the age of ten, and she couldn't help giving them some thought. They were healthy, pretty young girls growing up in a fast-growing, dynamic city, the capital city in a brand-new state. Catherine would have watched the fine coaches moving about town with their newly wealthy owners inside, and she couldn't help but consider that her daughters would not be without prospects as they came of age. Catherine was a religious woman, and worldly thoughts such as these she would have kept to herself, but she very well may have had them on behalf of her daughters.

She understood her husband, though. She had no doubt heard him talk of the benefits of owning land that would generate food and a steady income, that would not be as subject to the vagaries of commerce as was the drayage trade, or as seasonal as the threshing business. She knew he was thinking of the children, too, if perhaps in a different way than she. These children would inherit the farm that he had in mind. He might have considered they could expand the family acreage with the profits thrown off by his initial 160 acres, his grubstake. Perhaps he planned that his son could help with farming the additional acreage, and that his daughters would, thereby, eventually be young women of property. Catherine may have had misgivings, but she knew her husband, and she knew how noble his intentions were. She knew this had always been his plan.

Johan began to make his preparations. Even though the land might be free, there was still money and property required to begin a farm. His business in St. Paul was perfect to provide some of the tools he would need: three powerful horses to pull the plows required to till the soil. He would also bring the milk cow the family kept, and with some camping gear and a stove they would have the rudiments necessary for survival until they could put up something sturdier in advance of winter. Little Sarah was just turning three years of age, and her sisters were only a few years older; it was going to require a good deal of planning to make sure they would have all they would need to survive.

Johan had made the trip overland back in 1857, but he was going to have to pay the extra money for the steamboat passage this time. There was too much to bring to consider going the cheaper way, the more difficult overland route. The trek the family had made five short years before in going from Woodford County to the Mississippi was not the same: they had more to bring this time, the roads were wet with snow melt and spring rains, and Minnesota was rougher and hillier than Illinois.

April was the time to go. They knew that. March was too early. Minnesota was too cold in March. Indeed, the river was often frozen. April would still be cool, but Johan knew he had much work to do when they finally arrived at their homestead, work that had to be finished before the snows began the next autumn.

The Kochendorfers and their five children left their home in St. Paul for the last time that April 1862, bringing with them their wagon and their three horses and their milk cow and their cooking equipment and a trunk containing their clothes and household items. They headed down the gradual hill to reach the boat landing. The children could have had little or no memory of farming life, and they probably looked at the whole thing as a great adventure. Indeed, their parents probably also thought of it that way. Aboard a steamboat for the first time in five years, it must have been thrilling to consider the prospects in front of them.

The steamboats that would have accommodated the Kochendorfers and others like them were large and roomy. These steamboats strained laboriously upstream against the swift Mississippi current and away from the St. Paul landing. A few miles up the

Mississippi they would come to the bluffs formed by the confluence of the Mississippi and the Minnesota, and they would make a left turn to head onto the Minnesota, and into the more open country of the Minnesota River valley.

Residents of the Twin Cities today know the Minnesota River to be somewhat different from the Mississippi and the St. Croix. The Mississippi and the St. Croix cut through sandstone and limestone, and descend rapidly. The descent through the rocks forms bluffs on either side, and the rivers occupy most of the area between the bluffs. The Minnesota is a different matter entirely. It descends slowly, making much longer, more gradual work of the descent from the continental divide, and because of this it has dug a wide, meandering valley in which the main channel of the river occupies only a small part. The valley is filled with swamps and backwaters and eddies that drain slowly, inexorably, back into the main channel. The distance from one side of the valley to the other is often greater than five miles, and—needless to say—the bottom of the valley near the river channel is subject to flooding.

This distinctive geology created the land that Johan Kochendorfer had laid claim to. His 160 acres would be on the north side of the massive valley just above the point where the Redwood River merges with the Minnesota on the south side. It was a plot of tolerably flat land set against the edge of the valley, but a careful thirty feet or so above the floodplain of the river. It was perfect: rich soil, and plenty of southwestern sun exposure.

Their steamboat would have made a series of stops along the way: Mankato, New Ulm, and Fort Ridgely. Fort Ridgely, a U.S. government post perched along the north edge of the river valley just past New Ulm, was built in 1853 to organize the reservation lands created by the 1851 treaties. It was not much of a fort by military standards, but it served the purpose of keeping order and enforcing the treaty provisions. The stop below Fort Ridgely might have allowed a few soldiers ashore.

The Kochendorfers were headed a little farther on, a little past the point on the River where Beaver Creek flows in to the river from the north, a little more than a dozen miles past the fort. The steamboat would make a last stop there on the north side of the river before turning back downstream, and at this point the three horses, the milk cow, the wagon carrying the trunks and the stove went ashore, along with at least seven passengers.

The Kochendorfers had a good deal of walking ahead of them to get to their land, and they decided they had better fortify themselves a little. The stove was taken down, and Catherine began preparing a lunch for the group.

A look around must have been somewhat comforting to these new arrivals from St. Paul. They knew that the other side of the river was the Indian reservation, and the prospect of living alongside these Indians with five young children must have given Johan and Catherine some pause. Yet looking back downstream and across the river they would have seen what was called the Lower Sioux Agency, the quasi-governmental outpost they understood was there to sell food and clothing to the Indians and the settlers. There were sturdy stone buildings there, and a saw-mill in back of the two-story agency building that, to them, must have hinted at civilization.

They could see activity on their side of the river as well, farmers working the land a little above their luncheon spot. They were not going to be lonely frontier farmers. There were going to be plenty of others to keep them company, and with many of them they knew they could speak in their "good old German."

The trip from just north of the mouth of Beaver Creek to the new Kochendorfer homestead was about eight miles, a tough trip that would be made on foot with the wagon filled with the family's possessions. They were heading northwest along the east side of the river, in the river valley, and the road and the land were rough. The woods were thick and dark; indeed, they still are. The Kochendorfers were headed for Middle Creek, but they had to cross a few other creeks first. These creeks that rush down the sides of the valley make for short but sharp ravines. The creek beds themselves are soft, and expose the black soil underneath.

Middle Creek flows into the Minnesota River from the east, very near where Rice Creek flows into the Minnesota River from the west.

The Kochendorfers would have been tired when they reached their destination, the Middle Creek settlement, part of a larger area called Flora Township, but they would have been happy with what they found there. Their closest neighbors were the Boelters and the Reyffs and the Schwandts. The Schwandts were a large farming family who had come even more recently from Germany. It must have pleased Johan and Catherine Kochendorfer to encounter a group of such like-minded folks.

The Schwandts, who lived just west of them, were a young group similar to the Kochendorfers. This must have been gratifying to Catherine. She knew it would be hard to keep a close watch on her five children, but she must have hoped that the adult Schwandts would be able to help with that. Mary Schwandt was a vibrant fourteen-year-old. She might be able to help with Catherine's four daughters. Young August Schwandt was roughly Johan, Jr.'s age, and if the two of them didn't get into too much mischief, they could keep each other company.

Johan must have been happy to meet fellow farmer Johan Schwandt. The two of them were on the western frontier, but neither of them was really a frontiersman. They were farmers—professional farmers. When done properly, farming is a technically demanding business involving considerations of biology, hydrology, and chemistry as well as the tricky financial business of choosing to grow and sell the right products at the right prices, and it would consume them both.

The Kochendorfers pitched a large tent on the family property to sleep those first few weeks. It must have felt good to Johan to think of the land beneath him that way: as his property. He might have talked quietly with Catherine those first few nights as they looked up at the stars across the river valley, talking out his plans and his dreams. He would need his rest though, because in the morning there would be much to do.

A couple weeks later, Catherine would sit down to write her sister Rosina in Illinois. "I wrote in my last letter that the next letter would not be mailed in St. Paul anymore," she told her sister. "The land here is wonderful, as good as we only hoped for. There are about

60 acres for planting and 100 acres of prairie. A creek is running through the acreage and close to the house there is a spring."

Catherine had sized up the farming community around them, and comments that they "are mostly all beginners here and the oldest settlers are only here between 2 and 3 years." Catherine held out the hope she and her sister might be re-united, perhaps in this new spot, and she writes "[Y]ou could come now and maybe would be our neighbors." She knew this was unlikely, but Catherine closes her short letter by asking for the next best thing: "I beg you, dear Rosina, don't give up on writing. Sit down and write a long letter."

Catherine's mention of "60 acres for planting" is worth a moment's thought. We can't know if all 60 acres were planted in 1862, but if they were, the work required would have been daunting. Johan would have had to break and turn over these virgin acres, hitching his horses to a heavy metal plow to do the work. Sixty acres is roughly fifty football fields. If each row of plowing were separated by a yard from the next row, each of these football fields would involve three miles of walking through freshly turned-over black dirt, struggling to keep the heavy plow positioned properly upright all the while. If crops were to be planted by the first of June, at least three and more likely four miles of this difficult plowing would have to be done every day—rain or shine!—for six straight weeks between late April and early June.

In addition to plowing up that prairie soil Catherine describes and putting in some crops, Johan would have to build his family a log cabin to replace the tent. It would be about a quarter mile from where the Schwandts were going to build their cabin. He couldn't go in for anything big or elaborate; he didn't have the time before winter. He also had to be practical as to location. He would have to cut down trees and shave them to produce the logs for the family cabin, and the logs would have to be hauled to whatever site he chose. He had only his eleven-year-old son to help with that. Johan decided to build his cabin close to the woods surrounding the nearby creek to keep the job of hauling the logs as easy as possible. This would prove to be a good, indeed a life-saving decision.

IV

By mid-year 1861, it was clear the Civil War was not going to end quickly or without a fight. Southern forces were ready, and much more spirited than Union forces, and they would not be easily defeated.

President Lincoln perhaps knew this, but he was not interested in offering his opinion on the outcome or the length of the war. He focused instead on the justness of the Union cause.

The president addressed the Congress by letter dated July 4, 1861, and read in special session the following day.[13] He needed a congressional authorization for money and troops—$400 million dollars and 400,000 men—but such an authorization was not really in doubt, and simply going through the motions of requesting the authorization was not enough of a challenge for this great lawyer. He laid out the case—meticulously, logically—for defending the Union against this "secession" of the southern states through this force of arms.

He began by making it clear that the attack on Fort Sumter in South Carolina was unprovoked, that the Confederates knew the Union garrison there was a token presence that in no way threatened or could threaten nearby South Carolinians. Southerners could, therefore, not claim "self defense." Lincoln also pointed out that his promise to the Southerners in his first inaugural address that "[Y]ou can have no conflict without being yourselves the aggressors" had been kept.

The second part of the speech is interesting to modern ears. Lincoln the politician believed that many residents of the southern states were not in favor of secession. He claimed that, in some states, these Union loyalists were perhaps even a majority. Using the nearby case of Virginia as an example, he claimed that the Virginia Statehouse was controlled by a majority of "professed Union men" at the time of the attack on Fort Sumter. He claimed that somehow the attack had caused them to join the secessionists, "and with them, adopted an ordinance for withdrawing the State from the Union." This is significant to Lincoln the politician because it suggests the majority of voters in Virginia were not in favor of secession.

"The people of Virginia have thus allowed this giant insurrection to make its nest within her borders," he asserted, "and this government has no choice left but to deal with it, where it finds it. And it has the less regret, as the loyal citizens have, in due form, claimed its protection. Those loyal citizens, this government is bound to recognize, and protect, as being Virginia."

The president, therefore, must protect his citizens—even those in the southern states—against this insurrection. "The Constitution provides that the United States shall guarantee to every State in this Union a republican form of government," he concluded, "But if a State may lawfully go out of the Union, having done so, it may also discard the republican form of government; so that to prevent its going out, is an indispensable means, to the end, of maintaining the guaranty mentioned."

Lincoln goes on to address the entire idea of secession, arguing that the States of the Union have no such right, for the simple reason that the several states are creations of the Union and not the other way around, and that they never had any independent legal existence (with the possible exception of Texas). "The original ones passed into the Union even before they cast off their British colonial dependence; and the new ones each came into the Union directly from a condition of dependence," he asserted. "Having never been States, either in substance, or in name, outside the Union, whence this magical omnipotence of 'State rights,' asserting a claim of power to lawfully destroy the Union itself?"

Secession is simply inconsistent with the Constitution, Lincoln argues, and with everything the Union had done on behalf of the states. "The nation purchased, with money, the countries out of which several of the States were formed. Is it just that they shall go off without leave, and without refunding?" He used Florida as an example, a state that had seceded a few months before. "The nation paid very large sums to relieve Florida of the aboriginal tribes. Is it just that she shall now be off without consent, or without making any return? The nation is now in debt for money applied to the benefit of these so-called seceding States, in common with the rest. Is it just, either that creditors shall go unpaid, or the remaining States pay the whole?

"Again, if one State may secede, so may another; and when all shall have seceded, none is left to pay the debts. Is this quite just to creditors? Did we notify them of this sage view of ours when we borrowed the money?"

Lincoln concluded with an argument that resonated with that Republican Party platform from that far away time of May 1860—how long ago it must have seemed to the president as he drafted the speech!—in which he equated the Union with progress, material and intellectual, for all. "It may be affirmed, without extravagance, that the free institutions we enjoy, have developed the powers, and improved the condition, of our whole people, beyond any example in the world." He used as an example his own armed forces. "[T]here are many single Regiments whose members possess full practical knowledge of all the arts, sciences, professions . . . known in the world; and there is scarcely one, from which there could not be selected, a President, a Cabinet, a Congress, and perhaps a Court, abundantly competent to administer the government itself." He acknowledged that this was also true of Confederate regiments.

"This is essentially a People's contest," he concluded. "On the side of the Union, it is a struggle for maintaining in the world, that form, and substance of government, whose leading object is, to elevate the condition of men—to lift artificial weights from all shoulders—to clear the paths of laudable pursuit for all—to afford all, an unfettered start, and a fair chance, in the race of life."

It was brilliant, both legally and philosophically. Lincoln got what he wanted—troops and money—from Congress. The war would be quite another matter.

Southerners were not persuaded by President Lincoln's legal reasoning. One headline labeled Lincoln the "Northern Baboon."[14] The newspaper columnists throughout the southern states gasped at the size of the authorization, which they saw as wasteful and "to be squandered in a vain attempt to subjugate the South."[15] Some scoffed at Lincoln's claim that a majority in certain Confederate states actually opposed secession, and others poked at Lincoln's legal reasoning, arguing that the colonies raised money to win the Revolutionary war and therefore were acting as sovereign states before the creation of the Union.[16]

The Confederacy was ready to take the fight to the Union forces. Less than three weeks after Lincoln's speech, at the first Battle of Bull Run, Union forces under the command of General Irvin McDowell were defeated by Confederate forces commanded by, among others, General Thomas Jackson. The Confederates put up such a spirited defense at one point during the fighting that their General soon became known as "Stonewall" Jackson.

Lincoln was disappointed with the results at Bull Run. He appointed George McClellan to replace McDowell and drill the new recruits flooding into Washington, D.C., and, initially, Lincoln was happy with McClellan's leadership. McClellan was an energetic thirty-four-year-old, a top West Point graduate, a superb administrator, and he organized supply lines and drilled the Union forces into shape. Lincoln and others were so impressed with McClellan that when the portly, seventy-five-year old general-in-chief, Winfield Scott—"Old Fuss and Feathers"—retired, they turned to McClellan to take this top spot.

Lincoln warned McClellan of the enormous amount of work required in adding to his duties this new post of general-in-chief. "In addition to your present command, the supreme command of the Army will entail a vast labor upon you," he told McClellan.

"I can do it all," McClellan told him.[17]

McClellan was slow getting started, however. Lincoln had declared that Union forces should begin a general advance by February 22nd of 1862—George Washington's birthday—but it wasn't until March that McClellan's forces actually began moving slowly toward Richmond, the Confederate capitol.

Lincoln began to find McClellan's deliberation exasperating. Out west, young General Ulysses Grant was routing and capturing Confederate forts with remarkable speed. When Grant's troops were suddenly attacked by Confederate forces along the Tennessee River at Shiloh and fought back gamely before suffering serious losses, the president was told he should relieve Grant of command. Lincoln refused. "I can't spare this man," he explained in deciding to stick with Grant, "he fights."

V

IF THERE WAS ONE ASPECT of the white man's world Indian tribal leaders understood as well or better even than the whites, it was war. The deprivations, the uncertainties—these they would have been able to grasp without difficulty.

The Indians understood that their "Great White Father" in Washington was no longer the complete master of his fate. War was an all-encompassing proposition, they knew, and the government should be expected to have to change its way of conducting business. The Indians living alongside the Minnesota River should expect things to change, they just didn't know exactly how.

Concerns and complaints regarding the treaty terms would have eventually found their way to Chief Little Crow's doorstep—and it was a doorstep. Little Crow's position as a leader of the Mdewakanton Sioux, serving as their leader at the treaty talks, made him an important person in the eyes of the U.S. government and its agents and traders. He lived now in a house, a two-story frame house and not a tepee, two miles north of the Lower Agency, a house built for him by the agents and their moneyed interests.[18] He was also given a wagon,[19] and he asserted he was going to take up farming.

The two political sides of Chief Little Crow: diplomat (left) and warrior (right).

This new house and wagon and farm are things that would not have endeared him to fellow tribesmen like Cut-Nose and Red Middle Voice, who clung to their ancient ways and deplored the idea of the life of a non-warrior.[20] It was the Indian agency policy of the U.S. government to offer free land and training and tools to those who wished to take up farming. Very few did, perhaps ten percent or so—a measure of Little Crow's declining influence, and one that Little Crow could hardly fail to notice.[21]

Little Crow must have had concerns over his leadership position. His tribesmen may have heard that back in 1858, Little Crow had been the guest of the leader of the white men, President Buchanan. They may have heard how Little Crow had affected white man's manners. They might have heard of, indeed they may have seen, Little Crow's black frock coat and velvet collar. This image of him may have even become a matter of conversation among his warriors, and Little Crow could not have known how much of this was in fun and how much was real resentment.

Then there was the matter of Little Crow's involvement with the treaties themselves. The Indians would naturally wonder as to the government's ability, during time of war, to meet the treaty terms, and they might have asked Little Crow about this. They could be understandably concerned as to whether they would be paid.

They could also wonder as to exactly how they would be paid. Shortly after President Lincoln got his authorization of money from the Congress on July 5, 1861, U.S. Treasury Secretary Chase issued fifty-million dollars in debt notes, payable—as usual—on demand and, at the holder's option, in either paper currency or in gold. This would prove to be impractical: the U.S. government simply didn't have the gold to redeem all the notes they were issuing to finance the war, and creditors during wartime often nervously demanded gold. By December 1861 the Treasury was nearly out of gold. The government began printing new, unsecured paper currency in February 1862. This new federal currency that was no longer exchangeable for gold was called a "greenback," and it was a derogatory term.

The treaties of Mendota and Traverse des Sioux, however, stipulated payment in gold. Would the government suspend this provision as well, and pay them in paper money?

These fiscal problems of the federal government would have been of considerable interest to the agents and traders at the Indian agencies along the Minnesota River. Their whole reason for being there, for trading with the Indians, was dependent on the U.S. government coming through with the yearly treaty payments. Perhaps, the traders might speculate, the annuity payment would be made in greenbacks rather than in gold. Perhaps it would be smaller than usual due to senior government claims. Or perhaps payment would simply be delayed or suspended until the war was over.

This uncertainty these traders would probably have communicated to the Indians who lived nearby, and the Indians would have understood. The Indians would understand the situation differently, however. The traders might see most clearly the financial uncertainty, the Indians perhaps the military uncertainty. Once war commenced, tribal leaders knew, the outcome could never be certain. If their treaty was with a government that could be defeated in battle and fail, then did they not have a potentially unenforceable treaty?

The yearly payment was due at Fort Ridgely in June of 1862. It did not arrive. The Indians had little in the way of stored provisions—their crop yields had been poor in 1861 due to a generally poor growing season. The crops of 1862 were looking very good, but they were not ready just yet,[22] and the Indians were hungry. They wanted to borrow against the payment that should have arrived.

Bishop Whipple described the cluster of Indians that began to gather about the Lower Agency, demanding food for their tribes. "I had never seen the Indians so restless."[23]

"The Indians had heard that they were not to receive their payment," the bishop recalled, and he tried to assure them they would. The bishop addressed one of the trader's clerks, and told the clerk that "Major Galbraith, the [U.S. government's] agent, is coming down to enroll the Indians for payment."[24]

The clerk, in the tradition of clerks everywhere, tried to impress upon the bishop that he knew better. "Galbraith is a fool," the clerk told the bishop. "Why does he lie to them? I have heard from Washington that most of the appropriation has been used to pay claims against the Indians. The payment will not be made. I have told the Indians this, and have refused to trust them."[25]

Bishop Whipple was taken aback. "I was astounded that a trader's clerk should claim to know more about the payment than the government agent," he wrote later. The bishop perhaps hadn't had enough dealings with trader's clerks.

This trader's clerk, for better or worse, was the representative, the front face, of the U.S. government—at least as far as the Lower Sioux tribes were concerned. It was easy for the Indians to not much like what they saw.

ON THE OTHER SIDE of the Minnesota River, in Flora Township, the excitement in and around the Lower Agency was not felt by young Mary Schwandt. She was living with her large family on their new farm, but she recalls that she was a strong, "well developed" fourteen and a half years old—and she was bored stiff.

It is easy to see why. She had only one sister, but her sister was married, pregnant, and planning to move out to a farmstead of her own. Mary had brothers, but they were younger: eleven, six, and four years of age. "It was a little lonely, for our nearest neighbors were some distance away," she recalled years later. (The Kochendorfer children lived only a quarter-mile away, but their oldest daughter Rosina was only nine years old.) "The country was wild, though it was very beautiful," Mary recalled. "We had no schools or churches, and did not see many white people, and we children were often lonesome and longed for companions."[26]

There were plenty of Indians nearby, of course, just across the river. They were mostly members of Chief Shakopee's tribe, but as Mary remembers it, "they were not company. Their ways were so strange that they were disagreeable to me. They were always begging, but otherwise were well behaved. We treated them kindly, and tried the best we knew to keep their good will."

"About the 1st of August," Mary remembered, "a Mr. LeGrand Davis came to our house in search of a girl to go to the house of a Mr. Reynolds, who lived on the south side of the river, just above the mouth of the Redwood [River], and assist Mrs. Reynolds with the housework. Mr. Reynolds lived on the main road, between the Lower and Yellow Medicine agencies. They kept a sort of stopping place for travelers . . . I begged my mother to let me go and take the place. She and all the rest of the family were opposed to my going, but I insisted, and at last they let me have my way."

This was a chance to escape the loneliness and drudgery of daily life on the farm and to see more people. Mr. and Mrs. Reynolds also were instructors at a small government schoolhouse there—it was almost too good to be true! The work was not an onerous thought for Mary. She was a very willing worker, and she thought of herself as very capable. "I do not think the wages I was to receive were any consideration; indeed, I do not know what they were. Mr. Davis said there were two other girls at the Reynolds house, and that the family was very nice."

Mary was sold on the idea. "My mother and sister seemed to feel badly about me going, but I was light-hearted," she wrote. "[I]t is not very far," Mary told them all as she prepared to leave, "and I shall come back soon."

MARY SCHWANDT WAS heading across the river to work for the Reynolds family near the Lower Sioux Agency. It was now early August, and the Indians nearby were anxiously awaiting the arrival of their yearly annuity payment. They were hungry, and they demanded to be given food.

Agent Galbraith, the U.S. government's Indian agent, was the man in the middle. He did not know the reasons for the delay of the annuity payment. If the government had decided not to make the payment, how is it he would not have been told by now? He had to feel he was on solid ground in assuming the payment was simply late—

there was a war on, after all—and he, therefore, did not see any reason not to advance the Indians food on the assumption the payment was coming. He agreed with the request made by the Indians at the Upper Agency, and the traders at the Upper Sioux Agency released some food.[27] Little Crow made the same request on behalf of the Indians around the Lower Agency, and Galbraith again agreed with Little Crow's request that food be distributed.

The Lower Agency traders refused. Exactly what the traders were thinking cannot now be ascertained. The Myrick brothers, Andrew and Nathan, were the two traders there and they were getting rich off this Indian trade, and it seems incredibly short-sighted of them not to realize they had to extend credit to the Indians. Perhaps they had talked themselves into believing no annuity payment was ever going to be made, so it was pointless to extend credit. Perhaps they had listened to some of Little Crow's warriors assert they should be given a hearing by the government and agent Galbraith concerning their grievances before any of the trader's money claims could be deducted from the annuity payment, and this might have worried the Myrick brothers. Perhaps they had heard that Fort Ridgely Captain Marsh had told the Indians the soldiers in the fort were not "collection agents for the traders."[28] Whatever the case, these traders did as nervous traders often do: they looked at the immediate problem of advancing goods to people who could not immediately pay, and they refused.

The folks who could speak the Sioux language and could translate into English the Indian requests for food were often missionaries, and they would translate the traders' replies back. At some point that August, a request for food was translated for Andrew Myrick, along with the observation that "they will starve if the [annuity] money doesn't come soon."

The story that survived for over fifty years before being put in writing is that Andrew Myrick told the translator that "So far as I am concerned, if they are hungry let them eat grass!"[29]

Notes

[1]Journals of the Lewis and Clark Expedition—Saturday, August 24, 1805.

[2]*Undaunted Courage*, by S. Ambrose, pp. 188-189.

[3]*The Duty of Citizens Concerning the Indian Massacre* by H.B. Whipple (1862).

[4]Ibid.

[5]Letter written by H.B. Whipple, Bishop of Minnesota to the president of the United States—March 6, 1862.

[6]Oehler, p. 64.

[7]*Cut Nose: Who Stands on a Cloud* by L.D. Boutin (2006).

[8]E.g., *Old Rail Fence Corners* (1914), pp. 94-97.

[9]*Minnesota in Three Centuries*, volume III by L. Hubbard & R.I. Holcombe (1908), p. 274.

[10]Oehler, p. 25.

[11]*The Sioux Uprising of 1862* by K. Carley, p. 10.

[12]Oehler, p. 23.

[13]Address to the U.S. Congress in Special Session—July 5, 1861.

[14]*Raleigh, North Carolina State Journal*, July 10, 1861.

[15]*Hillsborough, North Carolina Recorder*, July 17, 1861.

[16]*Richmond Dispatch*, July 8, 1861.

[17]*Lincoln and the Sioux Uprising* by Hank H. Cox (2005), p. 59.

[18]*A History of the Great Massacre by the Sioux Indians* by C.A. Bryant (1864). Helen Carrothers's narrative describes Little Crow's house.

[19]Oehler, p. 15.

[20]Oehler, p. 21.

[21]Oehler, p. 16.

[22]*Through Dakota Eyes*, edited by G.C. Anderson and A.R. Woolworth. Big Eagle's Narrative 1, p. 26.

[23]*Light and Shadows of a Long Episcopate* by H.B. Whippple (1899) – Chapter 10.

[24]Ibid.

[25]Ibid.

[26]*The Story of Mary Schwandt* (1894), Minnesota Historical Society Collections.

[27]Carley, p. 5.

[28]Oehler, p. 26.

[29]*History of Minnesota* by W. Folwell (1924). It was Folwell who attempted to find a contemporaneous written recording of this encounter by someone with first-hand knowledge, without success. See *Minnesota History*, Spring 1983 issue, p. 198-206.

MINNESOTA: AUGUST 1862

I

RED MIDDLE VOICE and his small group of "trouble-makers" had no use for the reservation boundaries created by the treaties; indeed, they could not really afford to obey them if they wished to live as "true" Indians. They perhaps felt the ceding of such vast stretches of land to the white men was ridiculous and unjust—how could the white men "own" the very earth that they all shared? But their way of life, their hunting and fishing wherever the hunting and fishing was good, made it imperative that the boundaries be ignored.

Leaving Chief Shakopee's tribal setting near the mouth of the Redwood was perhaps driven by the desire to preserve their old ways. To truly leave the "captive" reservation setting and express their independence also meant of necessity that they leave the ten-mile-wide reservation on the south bank of the Minnesota to do their hunting and fishing.

They would live there as they had always lived. However, if the hunting and fishing didn't go well—what then? That was a problem, of course, which in times gone by would have resulted in disappointment, but not in frustration or anger.

Around midday on August 17th, four young braves from Red Middle Voice's group were returning from just such a hunt.[1] They stopped at a "General Store" near present day Acton, Minnesota. They were hungry and thirsty, and they demanded to be served. This demand was made of the proprietor, a fellow of the name Robinson Jones, who knew them and who the young braves knew. He refused to serve them, probably because he knew or felt strongly that the braves had no money.

He left the store in the care of his assistant and headed for a farm nearby where his wife was visiting her son by a previous marriage, and the young Indians followed him. Despite his refusal to serve them, the accounts of the events suggest that the braves engaged in conversation with Jones and were not threatening. When they arrived at the farm, the braves continued to talk pleasantly with Jones, his wife, his son-in-law, and a visitor and his wife from Wisconsin who were looking for a good patch of land to homestead.

The braves challenged the white men there to a gun shooting contest, and both groups fired a round at a target on a nearby tree. The white men did not immediately notice the braves re-loading the guns they held, and moments later the young Sioux braves opened fire on the white settlers. Suddenly Jones, his wife, his wife's son, and the young Wisconsin visitor were dead. Left frightened inside the house were the son's wife and the visitor's wife.

The braves fled, and as they did, they passed by the General Store and Clara Wilson, the fifteen-year-old girl Jones had left in charge of the store. Perhaps she approached them to ask when Jones was to return, or perhaps they thought she could identify them, or perhaps they feared she had heard the shots from half a mile away and was now armed. In any case, they shot Clara Wilson dead.

This, the braves knew, was an emergency. They "hitched up a team" of horses "belonging to another settler" and headed back home, to the Soldiers' Lodge alongside Rice Creek, and told Red Middle Voice and the others what they had done.

MARY SCHWANDT WROTE YEARS later that there was no church in the farming area around Flora Township. The development of these farmlands in 1862 was so new that the religious settlers hadn't had time yet to erect a building in which to hold worship services. This was not much of a problem for these new farmers, however. Nearly all of them were Protestants, like the Kochendorfers, and very comfortable with the idea that worship could be conducted anywhere, including out in the open under God's own beautiful and benevolent sky.

As these grisly, violent events were occurring just north of them, much of the Flora Township farming community was gathered for a worship service at the house of John Lettou, a service conducted by the Reverend Louis Seder. Reverend Seder lived in New Ulm, the town just south of the River near Fort Ridgely. He would travel upstream these thirty miles every few months to conduct worship services for these immigrant families in these new farming areas.

On this Sunday, August 17th, the Reverend Seder was presiding over two services for a total of over one hundred worshipers, and among the attendees were the Kochendorfers. Catherine would have insisted on their attending, of course. This was the chance that she and these other isolated farm families had to feel a little of the civilization that the church—in whatever building—represented, and they simply weren't going to miss their chance. There would be baptisms, perhaps even a wedding, and the idea of missing such events amidst the lonely drudgery of frontier farming life was unthinkable.

John Lettou's house could not accommodate the entire crowd of worshipers that Sunday. The women and girls would get the good spots inside the house where they could listen closely to the Reverend Seder. The men and boys would remain outside, near the open doorway, catching a few words now and then and perhaps looking around at intervals to gauge the weather for the trip home.

The Reverend Seder was a very popular figure among these farming families, and he would be entertained by them at their homes after the service. It was too long a trek back to New Ulm to risk starting in the late afternoon or evening, and Reverend Seder planned to spend the night at the Lettou house.

THE BRAVES HEADED BACK to their village near Rice Creek, forty long miles from Acton, and on arriving, they quickly told Red Middle Voice what had happened.

Red Middle Voice did not look at this as a simple matter of unprovoked murder. There were all kinds of considerations. The whites would come after him and his small tribe; that much was clear. Would he give up these four young braves to the white man's justice? Why? Would he give them up if they had killed other Indians, perhaps Chippewa Indians? Of course he would not.

He and many of his tribesmen, including the four braves, decided to talk to Chief Shakopee. They knew Shakopee disliked the whites. He would know what to do and would see their point that it was unthinkable to turn their braves over to the white men.

Chief Shakopee, when told what had happened, perhaps thought to himself that this was precisely the sort of difficulty that could be expected of Red Middle Voice and his motley group, but he listened and thought about the fix they were in.

As much as none of them wished to admit it, this was a problem for all of them living on the reservation near the Lower Agency. The white men, they knew, were sticklers for getting to the bottom of things, and there was nothing they liked getting to the bottom of more than an act of Indian violence such as this. All of them would also suffer some guilt by association with the young braves who had done the killing—they knew that. Chief Shakopee knew this was a problem for all of them.

The chief also knew his tribe was only a small part of the larger Indian community gathered along the river near the Lower Agency, and the real leader of that community—for better or worse—was Little Crow.

Some hundred or so anxious warriors proceeded south to Little Crow's house. It was early morning now, and these warriors, led by Chief Shakopee and Red Middle Voice, demanded to see Little Crow.

Little Crow heard his fellow tribesmen out. The men reviewed for him the events of the day before, and asked what they should do.

"Why do you come to me for advice?" he reportedly asked them all. "Go to the man you elected speaker and let him tell you what to do."[2]

This was a somewhat sullen reference to an election that Little Crow had lost recently to another of the Lower Sioux chiefs for the position of tribal spokesman.

"Little Crow is the greatest among the chiefs," answered Red Middle Voice. "Where he leads, all others will follow."

"What do you want?" Little Crow finally asked them.

"They want to kill all the whites," Red Middle Voice said, referring to the warriors still outside the house chanting in the twilight. "They want to drive them from the valley and get back our country."

"Red Middle Voice is a fool," Little Crow told them all.

This was a challenge, and Red Middle Voice laid out his case for war. "All the white soldiers are in the south fighting other white soldiers," he argued. "The Americans are so hard pressed they must take half-breeds and traders' clerks to help them with the fighting." Red Middle Voice could not resist concluding "[W]e have no choice," he said, although it might have been unclear who exactly he meant by 'we.' "Our hands are already bloody."

The arguing went on into the evening. Many of the chiefs knew that what was proposed was madness, and that the whites had cannons and much more ammunition than they did. Those who had traveled east knew when the whites mobilized to send more troops into the valley they would be vastly outnumbered.

The spirit of the young braves chanting outside was obvious, but the discretion of the chiefs still held the upper hand. Red Middle Voice summoned his courage, and he confronted the others, especially Little Crow, with a call that echoed through the generations of Sioux warriors. "Listen to the voice of the young men. They want to kill. If the chiefs stand in the way, they will be the first to die."

Little Crow knew he had to match this challenge. "Dakota chiefs do not fear to die. They will do what is best for their people, not what will please young braves and fools. What you propose is madness."

Red Middle Voice stepped closer and glared at Little Crow. "Little Crow is afraid of the white man. Little Crow is a coward."

Little Crow rose to his full height, stared back, and pointed to the scalp locks on the lodge poles around him, and refuted the charge that he was afraid, or a coward. "You know not what you are doing. You are full of the white man's devil water," he told them, but he was only getting warmed up. "We are only little herds of buffaloes left scattered; the great herds that once covered the prairies are no more. The white men are like the locusts when they fly so thick that the whole sky is a snowstorm. You may kill one, two, ten, yes, as many as the leaves in the forest yonder, and their brothers will not miss them, and ten times ten will come to kill you.

"They are fighting in the south. Do you hear the thunder of their big guns? No! It will take you two moons to run down to where they are fighting, and all the way you would be among white soldiers as thick as the tamaracks in the swamps of the Chippewas. Yes, they fight among themselves, but if you strike one of them, they will all turn upon you and devour you."

Little Crow had told them what he knew about the vastness of the white man's world east of them, and they were temporarily cowed, but Little Crow was looking around and thinking. Perhaps he was thinking about his role as leader, about the futility of holding on to their traditions in this white man's world. Little Crow had seen all these new settlers moving all along the opposite bank of the River, carving the land up, felling the trees, and he knew he had been present, and complicit, when that land was lost without a fight.

And the treaty terms, and Little Crow's not entirely innocent participation in creating them—where was the money that was due them? The treaties were a trick—it was all so easy to see that now! The nice, comfortable four walls around him might have suddenly seemed part of the trick, part of the white treachery! The whites had gotten them to surrender their lands without a fight, all because Little Crow and the other "leaders" became mesmerized by the white wealth and the white ways. Little Crow knew the chiefs and his warriors were thinking along these lines; they didn't actually have to say it. Could Little Crow not see their frustration, and could he feel that frustration, too?

"Fools!" he yelled out finally. "You will die like rabbits do when the hungry wolves hunt them." Then, suddenly, he announced his decision. "Little Crow is no coward. He will die with you!" The chiefs yelled and began chanting in unison with the young warriors outside.

Meanwhile, puttering down the road between St. Paul and Fort Ridgely was a wagon containing a heavy, well-guarded bit of cargo: two boxes, containing a total of a little over 200 pounds of solid gold, gold worth some $71,000 at the statutory conversion rate—the annuity payment for the year.[3] The U.S. government was somewhat late, but it was making good on its treaty promises. The gold had arrived in St. Paul on the 16th, but without telegraph lines between St. Paul and Fort Ridgely the people most interested in this development had no idea the yearly annuity payment was on the way.

II

That Sunday the 17th was memorable for the Kochendorfers. The formal worship service presided over by the minister from New Ulm was something they would have looked forward to. It gave them a little break from the endless work of getting their young farm into shape, and allowed them to see and greet their neighbors leisurely. Catherine would get a chance to relax a little bit and speak with the other women in her comfortable old German, and she must have also enjoyed showing off her four beautiful young daughters.

Late in the day something odd happened, however. One of the Indians came by the Kochendorfer cabin with some of his young braves. Rosina recalls that they explained "that they were going to fight the Chippewas, and were afraid their goods would be stolen by the enemy." It was a strange and somewhat worrisome request, but Johan and Catherine agreed, "and they were allowed to conceal beneath our beds their tomahawks and other articles of warfare."[4]

Johan had tried to learn a little of the language, but he had questions that he must have wanted to ask but was perhaps uncertain or unable to ask. How sure were the Indians of this planned attack? And if they wished to leave these weapons at the Kochendorfer house, did that mean that the fighting might follow right to their doorstep? This was a fearsome thought to parents with five children.

The next morning started out as it usually did, however. It was dry, and Johan set about "haying." Haying involved either cutting long wild grass or stacking and drying the cuttings, and in 1862 it was back-stiffening work done with a scythe. In August it was best done early in the day, before the sun made the work any more sweat-inducing than it had to be. It was a harvesting of sorts, but one that would feed only the livestock and not the farmer himself.

Around ten o'clock, Margaret remembered that "an Indian who had been friendly to us before this" came by the Kochendorfer cabin, "and had a bread and milk lunch." Margaret did not record the name of this Indian, but it may very well have been Cut-Nose, and it may have been the same warrior who the day before had asked them to store their "articles of warfare." Rosina remembers that "an Indian wearing a belt of cartridges and carrying a gun came to the house. Before this we had seen red men armed only with bows and arrows." Young Johan remembered that "The Indian had a gun in his hand, which he stood near the corner of the house outside."

By late morning Johan was finished cutting and stacking hay, and went inside their small cabin, and Catherine served him the same bread and milk. He was resting when Rosina ran in to announce that there were a large group of Indians outside, and that they were eating the turnips the family had planted. Johan rose and went outside.

Sure enough, there was a group of Indians a little distance from the house. One of the Indians near the cabin tossed the Kochendorfer axe into some shrubs near the woods behind. Young Johan watched this happen. "Although I was a boy of but eleven years" he wrote, "I noticed that something was wrong and called my father's attention to what the Indian had done. My father then went out and brought back the axe."

Father walked deliberately back in front of the house to where Rosina was standing on a bench to look out at the Indians in the field. He now stood between the Indians and his family.

Johan placed his arm on his daughter Rosina's shoulder and looked out at the group of Indians taking the turnips. Margaret then recalls that "the Indian who we had entertained earlier shot him in the back."

Johan slumped downwards. "He fell to the ground," Rosina recalled, "carrying me down with him." Rosina righted herself and ran away from the blast and her falling father and back inside the house, horrified.

The girls all crawled under a bed, but a short while later Rosina said to the other girls that "they will find us here." They all agreed to run out of the house, all but three-year-old Sarah, who "said she would stay with Mother." They ran out the door and looked down at their father.

Father looked up at his children. "He could not talk," Margaret recalls, "so he just beckoned us with his arms to go to the back of the house." Rosina quickly did as commanded, and seconds later Margaret and Catherine followed. They in turn may have yelled for Sarah to follow, but Sarah could not. Sarah was with her mother, with the mother who had always kept her safe.

"Our mother, standing at the corner of the house," Rosina recalls, "her arms up, screaming, was the last sight we had of her."

The girls ran into the woods, confused. Margaret was the last to leave her father, and as she ran into the woods a young Indian brave threw a piece of wood at her that hit her in the ear as she struggled over some logs in her path. The girls ran a ways into the woods, and a little later met up with their older brother, who had run around the house in the other direction. The girls wondered if they should wait awhile in the woods and then go back home. Young Johan had to tell them the bad news: Mother and Sarah were dead, too.

It had all happened so suddenly. The four children—Johan, Jr., Rosina, Catherine, and Margaret—looked at one another in horror through the woods. Young Johan remembers watching from the woods as one of the Indians grabbed a long sharpened wooden pole that his father had used to pack dirt tightly around fence posts. Johan watched and believed he saw the Indian raise the wooden pole high above his father's body and plunge it downward into his father's chest.

The children gathered together and ran away from the cabin. Their first confused thought was that this was all some terrible mistake, that perhaps they could run to a neighbor's house and the adults there could straighten it all out. It was all so confusing! What had happened? All they really understood was that something terrible was happening. Indeed, it was terrible.

THE KOCHENDORFERS COULD not know it, but a war had been declared by Little Crow and his warriors. Earlier that day, Little Crow led a large group of Indians in an attack on the settlements in and around the Lower Agency. In so doing, Little Crow's group was taking on their true enemies, the traders who thumbed their noses at them and had refused to give them food.

One of the Myrick clerks at the Lower Agency was an Indian scholar of sorts, James Lynd, who had learned the language as well as any of the traders and was writing a book describing their traditions and customs. He was leaning against the doorway of the trading post and was shot dead just as the Indians arrived.

Nathan Myrick was not at home, but Andrew Myrick was upstairs when he heard the shooting and commotion below. He suspected the worst, for he knew better than anyone the provocation the tribe had experienced. He went out a second floor window, slid down the lightening rod, and attempted to run for the woods, just as the Kochendorfer children had done. He was a marked man, however, and the distance was too great. He was shot dead before he could reach the woods.

Some who came upon his body later that day say they found his mouth stuffed with grass. Others said that as they passed through the area in flight to Fort Ridgely they saw a "sutler"—a trader—from the Lower Agency store, Andrew Myrick perhaps, who they came upon "lying face downwards, with a board on his back on which was written 'Feed your own squaws and papooses grass.'"[5]

The traders and their clerks were the first targets, but the killing spread. The Lower Agency physician and much his family, the superintendant, the ferry operator attempting to shuttle people across to the north side of the river—all were killed. A total of thirteen people lost their lives at the Lower Agency.

Cut-Nose and Red Middle Voice and their braves had not been in the group that attacked the Lower Agency. They had crossed the river to attack the settlements in Flora Township, killing farmers and women and children such as Johan and Catherine and Sarah Kochendorfer. Perhaps they felt the true enemies were these recent settlers, the people who were making exclusive use of what only four years before had been Indian land held by all, or at least all Indians of their tribe. These warriors could tell themselves that they were simply reclaiming ownership of these lands.

Red Middle Voice and his group attacked the Schwandt family,[6] and the killing they carried out there was too gruesome to document here. They shot Johan Schwandt, who was shingling the roof of the family cabin, then his wife, their daughter and her husband and their two youngest sons. August Schwandt, the twelve-year old, was attacked and was assumed dead, but he regained consciousness and reached cover.

Mary Schwandt was working at the Reynolds' house across the river, very near the Lower Agency. She and the Reynolds family heard the commotion in and around the agency. They piled onto the family wagon, and went quietly past the Lower Agency, stopping long enough to creep up to a ridge to take a look at the bloodshed and the carnage and at the buildings being set on fire. They made it past the agency undetected, and got within a few miles of New Ulm on the south side of the river before they were confronted by a large group of Indians heading back north. Mary was captured and held by the Indians.

Whether or not settlers were destined to survive that day had much to do with the specific group of Indians they encountered. In Flora Township, specifically the row of farms leading away from the river along Middle Creek, the Schwandt and Kochendorfer neighborhood, the attacks by Cut-Nose and Red Middle Voice and their warriors were truly frightening. Minnesota historian Marion Satterlee described it as "veritable slaughter fields."[7]

The Reverend Louis Christian Seder and the Lettou family were enjoying one another's company that Monday morning when news of the attacks reached them. They quickly prepared to leave, to head south and east towards Fort Ridgely and New Ulm, where Pastor Seder had his home. They encountered Indians as they made their way southeast, and Seder, John Lettou, and one of Lettou's young sons were immediately killed.[8]

There were eleven members of the extended Boelter family who lived on their large farm nearby, and seven were killed by Cut-Nose and his warriors. One of the Boelter men who was stabbed by Cut Nose clutched at him and bit one of the Indian's thumbs nearly off his hand just before dying.[9]

THE U.S. GOVERNMENT lumbered slowly and ineffectively to action. The men at Fort Ridgely began receiving refugees from the settlements below. The commanding officer was Captain John Marsh, a Minnesotan with a good Civil War record but no real frontier fighting experience. He had roughly eighty enlisted men under his command that Monday morning, and he decided to lead roughly half of them down the hill to the river and make a reconnaissance and perhaps quell the disturbance at the Lower Agency, the area that appeared to be the source of the trouble. Left in charge of Fort Ridgely was a nineteen-year-old lieutenant, Thomas Gere, along with thirty or so soldiers, a doctor, and an ordnance officer.

It is about a four-mile walk from the fort to the ferry crossing that leads to the south side of the river and the Lower Agency, and as they neared the crossing they could see dead bodies, and they could see smoke billowing from the burning agency buildings.

When they reached the crossing area, they saw an Indian on the opposite side, an Indian they trusted named White Dog, and he was motioning to them. Exactly what message he was trying to convey, whether to cross or not to cross, was unclear. Captain Marsh could not decide what to do, and as he considered his options a shot rang out.[10]

At this point all hell broke loose. The Indians were all around them, and they opened fire. Many of Marsh's men were sitting ducks. The soldiers fought their way to some dense brush alongside the river, which was somewhat swollen with summer rain, but there were Indians everywhere. Captain Marsh decided to make a break for the south side of the river, but he drowned.

Some fifteen men made it back to the shore on the north side, somewhere downstream. They struggled back to the Fort. Eight additional men from the party also survived and made it back slowly over the next few hours. Half the men in Captain Marsh's party were lost, a total of twenty four including the captain, and an additional five soldiers were badly injured.[11]

The killing along the Minnesota River that dreadful Monday was terrible, but by the horrific standards of the Civil War raging to the south and east it was not significant. The difficult thing for the whites was the details of the killings. Many more could be described here, but will not be. These stories have been recited before, and those interested can have no difficulty in accessing the accounts and reading of them to their heart's content. This chronicler is interested in telling a different sort of story, one less well-documented.

LITTLE CROW WAS RIGHT, HOWEVER. The white men "as thick as tamaracks in the forest of the Chippewas" would take notice, and would respond. It would take days—weeks, really—but the U.S. government, Abraham Lincoln's government, was now on notice and rising slowly to the challenge.

III

THE FOUR KOCHENDORFER CHILDREN tried to orient themselves in the woods behind the family cabin. "By this time the rest of the Indians had arrived and were running here and there looking for us," Rosina remembers.

What should they do? They had to worry that the Indian warriors would come after them. Why would these Indians bother to kill their parents and sister if they didn't also want to kill them as well?

It was so frightening. The woods were thick and dark all around them, and they knew it provided them cover, but they also knew this meant they couldn't see the Indians or anyone else approaching them until they were very close. Johan tried to keep his sisters quiet and to keep them from crying, because others could hear their cries and because in silence they might be able to hear others before they could see them.

Johan had the idea they might go to see one of their neighbors. Perhaps one of their trusted neighbors would know what to do. He knew the way to one of their neighbor's cabins quite well. It was down near the river bottoms, and he knew the way because he helped his father farm some of the land nearby. The girls followed him, and he motioned for them to keep quiet, but as they approached the neighbor's property— it may have been the Schwandts, whose cabin would have been west of them, in the direction of the river bottoms—they could hear gunshots and Indian war yells. From the bluff overlooking the neighbor's farmhouse the children could see the Indians.

The Indians were attacking and killing their neighbors, too!

Good Lord—what to do? Johan must have wiped away tears as he looked out at the farmhouse and the carnage and then around at his three little sisters and thought how hopeless it all was. How could he keep them safe? The girls were so small, and so fretful, and they were crying. What on earth to do with them?

Johan remembered something his father told him. The road to Fort Ridgely, the path to take to go south and east along the edge of the river valley—he remembered the way. Maybe, just maybe, they could stay in the woods near the road, escape detection, and make their way gradually to the fort. Fort Ridgely, his father told him, was filled with soldiers, government soldiers. They would certainly be able to help him and his little sisters, wouldn't they?

He told his sisters his plan. "Father had once pointed out to Johan the direction of the New Ulm road," Rosina recalls, "from which, some distance on, the Fort Ridgely road branched off across the prairie."[12] Johan knew it was a long way to Fort Ridgely; his father may have mentioned the distance at over twenty miles. It would have been foolish to discourage his sisters at this point, however.

At first they kept to the woods, but it was slow going. The woods there are filled with thick underbrush, and the thorny bushes scraped their arms and legs. Johan knew they were not making good progress, that they weren't going nearly fast enough. The woods along the path were on a mild hillside, too, and the footing was uncertain and frustrating. Their fright subsided a little with time, and as they looked around some more and down at the road, they noticed a better, easier way to make the long walk.

"The grass was a yard high beside the road," Margaret remembered. They decided to try to walk along the more open and level ground alongside the road while remaining concealed in the long grass. "So whenever we saw or heard anything we would hide in the grass till it was safe to go on," she wrote.

They walked this way for miles that warm August day, constantly looking in all directions, ready to flee into the woods at any sign of Indians. It was exhausting. "As we walked on we heard now and then the sound of guns, and we hid in the long grass until we felt that the danger had passed," Rosina remembered.

They had been hours walking when all four of them saw a man approaching them from behind. He was a distance away, walking along the road with a dog beside him. The girls ran into the grass in fear, thinking this was perhaps the end.

Johan watched closely from the grass, and as the man got closer he could get a better look at his clothes and his manner. "He is not an Indian," he told his sisters. It was Mr. Michael Boelter, their neighbor, one of the other members of their church. In Michael's arms was a six-month old child, Michael's nephew Julius.

The Kochendorfer children told him their story. Michael listened, and told them they were doing the only thing they could do—get to Fort Ridgely. He himself was doing the same thing, heading for the Fort, hoping against hope that his six-month-old nephew could survive the journey.

Michael was thirty-one years old, and earlier in the day he had been a married man and father of three, a member of a large extended farming family of eleven. On returning to the farm that morning after having run an errand, he had found nearly all of them dead, killed by the same Cut-Nose and his group. It was probably Michael's brother John, young Julius's father, who had been stabbed to death and who had nearly bit off the thumb of Cut-Nose, his attacker, as he struggled with him.[13]

Michael told them that there was a larger group coming up behind them, a family of survivors traveling by wagon. Michael told the children if they made it to Beaver Creek before the wagon caught up to them they should wait there, where the wagon would surely slow down for a while and perhaps stop for water.

The children had already gone some ten miles, and Johan knew that Beaver Creek, the largest and the widest of the many creeks that ran down the hills of the valley, was still a good mile or two further. He didn't mention this to his young sisters, however—what else was there to do but to walk and to try to survive?

The children were by now very tired and hot and leg weary, but they were thirsty, very thirsty, too. The idea that their destination was a place with cool water in the bottom of a nice, shady creek bed probably drove them on a little. They could have decided to sit still in the long grass and wait for this wagon that Michael Boelter told them was coming, but how sure could anyone be about something like that? Indeed, how sure could anyone be about anything that day? It was better to press on for Beaver Creek.

It would be another half hour before they would reach their destination. The path they were on was in the direct line of the late afternoon sun. They were tired, exhausted by the combination of fear and hunger and endless walking through the brush and the tall grass.

Yet they did reach Beaver Creek late that day, eleven miles from where they had started behind their parent's cabin. Sixty years later,

Margaret would recall it all. "I'll never forget how good the water tasted when we got to the creek," she wrote.

Margaret could recall no more of that day and what happened after this, however. After she drank as much as she wanted from the water in Beaver Creek she immediately fell fast asleep!

Her brother and older sister Rosina probably looked at their little sister and knew they didn't have the heart to wake her. Why? They kept an eye on her, perhaps understanding they had to let her sleep alongside the creek bed while she could, for they couldn't know for sure what was in store for them next. They waited, just as Michael Boelter had told them to.

Sure enough, a little while later, wagons driven by ox teams were seen coming down the road from the west. It was a real troupe, eight members of the Lenz family that had farmed in the same area around Middle Creek. The Lenz wagons were nearly full, but the family must have looked down at these four Kochendorfer children and known that they had to find room for them somehow. Johan probably would have hoisted his little sister Margaret, fast asleep, into a wagon.

It was dusk when they left Beaver Creek, and it must have been worrisome to no longer be able to see much in front of them. The folks in those wagons couldn't help but imagine the worst around every bend; indeed, earlier that day most of them had seen the worst. Still, it must have been a relief for Johan and Rosina to be able to look around and know that their two little sisters were not so completely dependent on them any more, that all four of them had the protection of adults again.

It is uphill all the way near the fort, and it must have been a relief to pull up to the front gate. It was the middle of the night, but at last they could stop moving and worrying about the next corner.

Rosina remembers what happened next. "At the gates of the fort we were refused admittance because the people within feared that the Indians would rush the gate were they to open it."

Fort Ridgely was at that moment manned by only about thirty healthy soldiers, and when these refugees arrived in the middle of the night, the soldiers could not be sure that by allowing the refugees in they would not leave themselves open to an attack by the Indian warriors. "So we slept under the wagons until next morning," Rosina recalled, "in peril of a possible night attack on the fort."

Margaret recalls waking early the next morning. "I never saw those people [who had picked them up], and never awoke till we were at the fort the next morning," she wrote.

The sun rose, and the gates were finally opened early that Tuesday morning, and the refugees from all around the river valley flooded inside the fort.

IV

IT MUST HAVE BEEN CHAOS. Two hundred, maybe three hundred utterly horrified and distraught refugees, most of them women and children, and only around thirty soldiers. Everyone was hungry, famished, but the fort had only the small kitchen and commissary sized for fifty or at most one hundred. The soldiers were still trying to understand what had happened to their commanding officer and their colleagues the day before near the ferry crossing.

Amidst all the chaos, the soldiers had to prepare the fort for an attack by the Indian warriors. They would be outmanned, and defeat would be catastrophic for them and for the refugees.

Word had been sent out in a couple of directions, asking for help. Captain Marsh had sent one of his men on horseback to try to re-direct a group of some fifty soldiers heading for a U.S. Army camp in northern Minnesota back to Fort Ridgely.

Later that Monday, when word reached Fort Ridgely that Captain Marsh and many of his men had been killed, nineteen-year-old Second-Lieutenant Gere realized he was in charge. Gere decided to put a letter describing the situation in the hands of a Private Sturgis, put Sturgis atop the best horse in the fort, and sent him off for Fort Snelling, 100 miles to the northeast. Sturgis was to ask for reinforcements and to notify Governor Ramsey in St. Paul of the attack. Sturgis was also to try to intercept a group of local Renville County volunteer soldiers, the Renville Rangers, who had just left for the Civil War, and re-direct them back to the Fort.[14]

By Tuesday morning the 19th—when the Kochendorfer children reached Fort Ridgely—none of these reinforcements had yet arrived when Little Crow and his warriors were spotted just outside the Fort. We know this from the recollections of one of the Fort Ridgely soldier's wives, Mrs. Margaret King Hern, whose husband had been sent off to the Civil War weeks before.

"About ten o'clock in the morning," Mrs. King Hern wrote, referring to that Tuesday the 19th, "Lieutenant Gere, a boy of nineteen, who was left in command when the senior officers were killed, called on me. On a hill to the northwest, a great body of Indians were assembled. He wanted me to look through the field piece and see if Little Crow was the leader. I knew him at once among the cavorting throng of challenging devils. . . . We watched them breathlessly as they sat in council knowing that if they came then we were lost. The council was long, but finally after giving the blood curdling war whoop, they rode away."[15]

Margaret King Hern's word choices echo down to us now like fingernails on a chalkboard. It is painful to read her characterizations of the Indian warriors. She lived in a different time and place, of course, and we should perhaps bear in mind that she had no doubt that her life and the lives of her young children were imperiled by those warriors.

Her words and observations are important, however. Historians now believe that what Mrs. King Hern was viewing through that field piece was Little Crow's loss of control of events and of the warriors of his nation. Little Crow advocated attacking Fort Ridgely, and in doing so he was acting as the leader of a nation at war attempting to directly confront and defeat the enemy. When his warriors decided instead to disband, with some of them deciding to cross the river to attack New Ulm, Little Crow was essentially being overthrown.[16]

By mid-day Tuesday, the fifty soldiers had been re-routed back to Fort Ridgely, and by late afternoon the Renville Rangers arrived from nearby St. Peter. Young Lieutenant Gere was relieved of command by twenty-five-year-old Lieutenant Timothy Sheehan, the officer in command of the soldiers who had been re-directed back to the fort.

Lieutenant Sheehan prepared Fort Ridgely and its ragtag occupants to defend the Fort. He rounded up the male refugees and equipped them with muskets, ordering the blacksmith to begin cutting up metal rods into makeshift slugs to supplement their ammunition. He positioned the cannons and organized the artillery men. He organized the other refugees into help groups and told the women and children where they must go in the event of an attack and remain until further notice.

Margaret Kochendorfer remembered many years later—with some pride I think—how she and her older brother and her sister Rosina helped Dr. and Mrs. Eliza Mueller, the Fort Ridgely doctor and nurse, by cutting cloth into bandages and how they served meals to the many refugees.

The Fort had no well or spring from which to draw fresh water, and on Tuesday and early Wednesday the refugees took turns driving the mule team down the hill leading to the river, drawing water from a spring near the river and hauling bucket after bucket of fresh water up the hill to make sure they could withstand a long siege.

Around 1:00 p.m. on Wednesday, the Indian warriors attacked Fort Ridgely from all directions. There were no defensible walls around the perimeter, so the Indians could quite easily get into shooting range of the buildings, and they did take control of a few buildings to the northeast. Lieutenant Sheehan and his men returned fire. The soldiers were outnumbered, but they were defending only a small area, and they were able to hold their lines and resist further advances.

Lieutenant Sheehan's ordnance officer, Sergeant John Jones, commanded his artillery men at intervals to let loose with a few rounds of their 6-, 12-, and 24-lb balls. They took close aim at the ravines at the edges of the hills leading up to the fort from the southwest, where they believed the Indians would be lying in wait between attacks. The warriors evacuated these areas, often retreating down the hill and away from the fight. The battle was over by dusk.

MRS. MARGARET KING HERN was the most colorful chronicler of those days at Fort Ridgely. As you might imagine, the wife of a soldier serving out on a frontier post like Fort Ridgely was no shrinking violet. When preparations for defense of the fort began in earnest on Tuesday, she wrote that she and one of the other wives, Mrs. Dunn, "had asked for guns to help fight, but there were none for us." They set about making cartridges. "We would take a piece of paper, give it a twist, drop in some powder and one of these slugs or balls, and give it another twist. The soldiers could fire twice as fast with these as when they loaded themselves. All the women helped."

On Wednesday, Mrs. King Hern described how "early in the afternoon the long expected fighting began. We were all sent upstairs to stay and obliged to sit on the floor or lie prone. All the windows were shot in and the glass and spent bullets fell all around us. I picked up a wash basin full of these and Mrs. Dunn as many more. By evening, the savages retired, giving their awful war whoops."

Mrs. King Hern wrote of the women refugees. "None of the women seemed to think of their wounds. They lamented their dead and lost," she observed. "The suffering of these women stirred me to the depths."

Mrs. King Hern described a mother distraught over the loss of her four small children who had scattered in all directions when the Indians attacked the family farm. The mother, having now made it to Fort Ridgely, feared that her children were all dead. "She would sit looking into space, calling 'Mine schilder! Mine schilder!' Enough to break your heart," she wrote.

"I thought she had gone crazy," Mrs. King Hern continued, "when I saw her look up at the sound of a child's voice, then begin to climb on the table calling 'Mine schilder! Mine schilder!' In a group on the other side she had seen four of her children that had escaped and just reached the fort that Wednesday morning."

The activity at Fort Ridgely that week was half military preparation for the coming attacks and half a sort of delirious summer roadside campground affair. Many of the children were unsupervised and they ran around everywhere, playing games by locking each other into root cellars and ice houses. Some found live cartridges and bags of powder to use as toys. Margaret Kochendorfer described how she and some other young children were picking hazel nuts among the hazel bushes in the woods on Thursday the 21st when the sound of gunfire caused her and the others to race back into the fort buildings.

"During the night," Lieutenant Sheehan wrote in his report concerning that Thursday night, "several people, remnants of once thriving families, arrived at the post in a most miserable condition, some wounded—severely burned—having made their escape from their dwellings which were fired by the Indians."

One of these would have been twelve-year-old August Schwandt. August was left for dead on the 18th when Indian warriors killed everyone else at his family farm. August found cover in the woods, and over the course of almost four days was able to make it the twenty-five miles from Flora Township to Fort Ridgely, with a deep wound to his head. Once at the fort, he probably had a chance to talk with his neighbors, and tell them of his ordeal and of the fate of their family.[17]

Meanwhile, Chiefs Shakopee and Mankato were agreeing to join forces with Chief Little Crow. Some 800 warriors were now going to try to take Fort Ridgely.

THE LETTER DISPATCHED with Private Sturgis on the 18th had reached Fort Snelling in only eighteen hours. Horses and weapons and equipment were assembled as Sturgis pressed on to deliver the news to Governor Ramsey in St. Paul. Governor Ramsey knew what to do: He would enlist the help of his old political rival, Henry Sibley. These were Sibley's people, Ramsey perhaps thought, people with whom

Sibley had been hunting and trading for decades. Sibley was not a military man, but Ramsey trusted he would know what to do.[18]

Sibley lived in retirement in his large stone house across the Minnesota River from Fort Snelling. He understood Ramsey's request. He knew the Indian leaders better than almost anyone else near political power in Minnesota. He may have even worried over the preceding months that something like this might happen when he read of all the homesteading being done on the former Indian lands along the Minnesota River. He agreed to take on the assignment, and Ramsey appointed him Major of a "Minnesota Militia" to be organized to fight the Indians. The announcement of the attacks was accompanied by a call for volunteers, and men from around the St. Paul area were signing up to fight.

Sibley went across the river to Fort Snelling, organized these volunteers, and headed down the road to Fort Ridgely. His pace was deliberate, filled with stops to gather information, almost as if he hoped the gradual realization of his presence in the Minnesota River valley would cause the Indians to cease hostilities.

There would be no such cessation. The warriors made their way up the sides of the hills leading up to Fort Ridgely on Friday the 22nd, preparing to attack from two sides. As to the details of what happened next, let's dispense with all the military mumbo jumbo and let Mrs. Margaret King Hern describe that dramatic afternoon:

"Friday was a terrific battle. A short distance from the fort was a large mule barn. The Indians swarmed in there. Sergeant Jones understood their method of warfare, so trained cannon loaded with shell on the barn. At a signal these were discharged, blowing up the barn and setting the hay on fire. The air was filled with legs, arms, and bodies and these fell back in to the flames. It was the soldiers who saved Minneapolis and St. Paul and the towns between, when the Indians failed to capture the fort."

These hundreds of Indian warriors had fought bravely, courageously, but they were facing with their few muskets and their bows and arrows the brutal, powerful weapons that would cause such carnage at Antietam and Gettysburg. They withdrew, but they were still willing to fight. They needed a new target, perhaps one without artillery.

The attack they made on New Ulm the following day was dramatic. They rushed the town in one large wave from the west, and their numbers were such that the 220-some men defending the town retreated from the western edge. The men defending then counter-attacked in small bands. It was when these defenders organized a rush upon a group of some sixty Indian warriors gathering along the river that they took the offensive, and the Indians retreated from the town with the sunset.[19]

The defenders of New Ulm assessed the damage to their town the next morning, and they had to concede that it was bad. Thirty-four men died defending New Ulm, and many of the buildings along the western edge of town were destroyed. There was almost no town left to defend by day break on Sunday.

The city fathers decided to abandon the town. Wagons were hastily assembled and the residents of the New Ulm area loaded onto them what they could salvage. They then began a long slow procession south and east, to the town of Mankato, thirty miles away, escorted by a force of soldiers newly arrived from St. Peter. "It was a melancholy spectacle," wrote Charles E. Flandrau, a lawyer from St. Peter who had rushed to New Ulm on the 19th along with a few hundred others and who then led the defense of the town, "to see 2,000 people, who a few days before had been prosperous and happy, reduced to utter beggary."

Notes

[1] Their translated names were Brown Wing, Breaking Up, Killing Ghost, and Runs Against Something When Crawling. The names and the details regarding these events were part of Big Eagle's Narrative 1 and appeared in *Through Dakota Eyes*, p. 35-36. The four young braves related the details regarding the events to Big Eagle.

[2] Collections of the Minnesota Historical Society. Big Eagle told of the details of these meetings with Chief Shakopee and the subsequent council at Little Crow's house. The confrontation between Little Crow and the men from the Rice Creek Soldiers' Lodge, as well as Little Crow's impassioned speech, was memorized and later described by one of Little Crow's sons, Wowinape.

[3]*Minnesota in the Civil and Indian Wars*, St. Paul Pioneer Press Co.—Account of Lt. Gere.

[4]Rosina's account appeared in the *St. Paul Pioneer Press*, August 15, 1926.

[5]*Old Rail Fence Corners*, edited by Lucy Leavenworth Wilder Morris (1914)—Account of Mrs. Margaret King Hern, Fort Ridgely soldier's wife.

[6]Cox, p. 51.

[7]*Massacre by Dakota Indians* by M. Satterlee (1923), p. 27. The shooting of Johan Kochendorfer, whose home was "some 80 rods [0.25 miles] away" from the Schwandt house, is described: "Kochendorfer was shot down in the dooryard, and the baby Sarah and the wife, in the house. The father lived long enough to direct his other three [s.i.c.] children to hide in the brush."

[8]Satterlee, p. 30.

[9]Satterlee, p. 29.

[10]Oehler, pp. 78-79.

[11]Carley, p. 16.

[12]*St. Paul Pioneer Press*, August 15, 1926. Much of Rosina's account of the events of that day is taken from this article.

[13]In making sense of the chronology, it could be that Cut-Nose led the attack on the Kochendorfers at about the same time that Red Middle Voice and his warriors attacked the Schwandts. If the Kochendorfer children, on fleeing, went to look down upon another farm family whose house was west of them and closer to the river bottoms, they would have perhaps been viewing the attack upon the Schwandts. Cut-Nose may have gone east of the Kochendorfer farm, toward the Boelters, and, therefore, in the direction opposite the Kochedorfer children. The Kochendorfer children would have then begun walking southeast toward Fort Ridgely somewhat before Michael Boelter fled the Boelter farm for Fort Ridgely. This would explain why it took Michael Boelter awhile to catch up with the Kochendorfer children.

[14]Carley, p. 26.

[15]*Old Rail Fence Corners*, account of Mrs. Margaret King Hern.

[16]See Oehler, pp. 92-95.

[17]Margaret Kochedorfer recalled in one of her letters that "a neighbor boy came and said he came to our house and found the Indians had torn up a quilt and tied Mother and Sarah together." This neighbor boy was probably August Schwandt.

[18]Carley, pp. 30-31.

[19]Minnesota historian William Folwell would write of the defense of New Ulm: "This was no sham battle, no trivial affair, but an heroic defense of a beleaguered town against a much superior force." *A History of Minnesota* (1924).

AFTERMATH

I

THE SITUATION AT FORT RIDGELY following the attacks on the 20th and the 22nd was also dire. Provisions were low, and the milk cows had been driven off. Margaret King Hern describes feeding her young children hard tack and bacon for ten straight days, chewing it a little first for her infant. She remembered the sanitation conditions, writing "no words I know could describe it." Many of the buildings were burned or destroyed. There were hundreds of women and children who had no business in such a hostile environment. The soldiers there could only hope that the Indian warriors would not attack again.

Colonel Sibley and his Minnesota Militia were headed for Fort Ridgely, but they were taking their time, gathering troops and weapons as they made their way slowly south. On August 28th, Sibley's 1,500 well-armed soldiers finally reached Fort Ridgely. Sibley and his men had turned the two- or three-day trek from Fort Snelling into an eight day affair. Sibley had devoted an entire day at Fort Snelling to documenting the additional provisions he wanted, and he remained another day in the town of St. Peter, waiting for additional troops and arms and cavalry and fresh intelligence on the location and strength of the Indian warriors.

Sibley ordered a military escort for the women and children at Fort Ridgely to a steamboat bound for St. Peter and St. Paul. The Kochendorfer children were among those packed onto wagons for the journey, and as they left the fort they were again in fear of an Indian attack upon the wagon convoy. No attack occurred, and they were put on board the steamboat *New Ulm*, heading north, downstream, for St. Paul.

The refugees at Fort Ridgely asked Colonel Sibley to send out a party to bury their dead relatives, and Sibley agreed. Captain Hiram P. Grant of the Sixth Minnesota Infantry led the group of fifty soldiers of his Company A, with the goal of making a general reconnaissance, picking up any settlers they might come across, and burying the dead. Company A, along with another hundred volunteers, left the Fort early the morning of August 31st.

It cannot have been a welcome task. The bodies had now been dead almost two weeks. The graves they dug were often shallow and unmarked. The party split into two groups, with many of the volunteers sent across the river to bury the bodies near the Lower Sioux Agency. Captain Grant stayed on the north side, and buried the bodies they found there.

Grant and the Sixth Minnesota Infantry and other volunteers were burying the bodies of Johan, Catherine, and little Sarah Kochendorfer just as the surviving members of the family—Rosina, Catherine, Margaret, and Johan, Jr.—were making their way overland and away from Fort Ridgely to St. Peter and then to St. Paul. Rosina, Catherine, and Margaret would never return.

Grant and his soldiers didn't want to travel all the way back to Fort Ridgely in the evenings, so they camped alongside the river. The evening of the 1st, they set up camp at a place called Birch Coulee, a creek north of the river and about fifteen miles from the Fort. Early on the morning of the 2nd they were attacked by Indian warriors. Thirty hours of fighting ensued before hundreds of troops from Fort Ridgely arrived to rescue their comrades. Dozens of soldiers and Indians were killed. All of Captain Grant's horses, almost one hundred of them, were killed during the fight.[1]

On September 6th, President Lincoln appointed Major General John Pope to lead the arriving U.S. government troops that would be sent to Minnesota to quell the uprising. Pope had led the Union forces in the second Battle of Bull Run only two weeks earlier, but at Bull Run his troops and his officers found he shunned responsibility for failures and they disliked him. Lincoln relieved him of command and dispatched him to Minnesota. Lincoln and his cabinet tried to impress upon Pope the importance of restoring order out in Minnesota, but Pope did not fail to recognize it as a demotion. He wrote of his "banishment to a distant and unimportant department."[2]

Distant and unimportant, perhaps, but in commanding a now overwhelming number of organized and armed Union and Minnesota Militia soldiers against a comparatively unarmed group of Sioux Indians, Pope was assured of a military success. It was difficult to get federal soldiers to make the trek to Minnesota, however. Soldiers who had been captured by the Confederacy and were sitting out the war as parolees, ineligible to fight the South again but perfectly eligible to be sent out west to fight Indians, generally weren't interested. These paroled soldiers were not interested in traveling hundreds of miles to fight Indians, perhaps for some of the same reasons Pope was not that interested. Whatever the case, Pope and his forces were largely irrelevant in the September offensive against the Indians. Hastily assembled Minnesotans under the command of Colonel Sibley and Charles Flandrau would do most of the fighting.

Sibley was shocked by what had happened at Birch Coulee, and he demanded better information regarding the location of Indian forces. This would take time, but Sibley considered time to be on his side. He may have been right, yet Sibley also knew that the Indians were holding hundreds of hostages—women and children like Mary Schwandt—who had been captured in the early days of the fighting.

Former frontiersman Henry Sibley set about communicating with his old business partner, Little Crow. He sent a note carried on horseback to the Indian camp, demanding Little Crow release the prisoners. Little Crow rebuffed him with a list of grievances. Sibley reiterated his request, demanding Little Crow behave like a leader, release the prisoners, surrender his forces, "and I will talk with you again like a man." Little Crow declined.

Sibley and his troops finally left Fort Ridgely on September 18th, and they slowly tracked the Indian tribes up the Minnesota River. His intelligence was that most of the Lower Sioux Indians had retreated north, to near the Upper Agency, along with their prisoners. The Upper Agency is some forty miles from Fort Ridgely. Sibley plodded deliberately north, fearing an ambush. He reasoned that he did not have enough scouts on horseback—most of the horses were killed at Birch Coulee—so he went slowly. Very slowly.[3]

Sibley and his soldiers made their way north along the west side of the river. They encountered few Indians on this slow march. They slowly approached the Upper Agency.

The Lower Sioux warriors could not rally many of the warriors near the Upper Agency, the Sissetons and the Wahpetons, to their fight. These two distinct groups of tribes had a very different view of things. The Sisseton and Wahpeton warriors may have been involved in some acts of violence, and they may have held hostages, but they hadn't committed wholesale massacres or directly attacked Union soldiers. This was not their fight.

The warriors had watched Sibley's troops advance along the river, and—led now in battle by Soldiers' Lodge members such as Cut-Nose[4]—they planned their attack. Early the morning of September 23rd, just south of the Upper Agency, and just as Sibley's troops prepared to eat breakfast and break camp, they launched their attack. Some of Sibley's lead soldiers furthest north were killed, but the Indians again had trouble remaining organized in the face of artillery fire. Many were unable to join in the attack before Little Crow and his warrior leaders abandoned the field.

This "Battle of Wood Lake" took place three or four miles south of the main Indian encampment, where the hostages were being held. Sibley again waited until he could gauge the enemy's strength near the encampment before proceeding.

Many of the Indian warriors took flight, but others did not. Cut-Nose considered flight futile, and announced to the others that he expected to be executed.⁵ Little Crow knew the fighting was over before Sibley did, and he and his young braves headed north and west.

The remaining Indians, roughly one thousand of them, surrendered when Sibley's forces finally reached them on the 26th. They released the hostages, hostages who in many cases had been captured and brought there by others who had fled the area. Sibley somewhat ceremoniously named the site Camp Release, and it is today the site of a Minnesota state park of the same name.

The hostages, some one hundred whites and two hundred "half-breeds," had had an awful time of it. One of the Minnesota volunteer soldiers was a St. Paul lawyer named Isaac Heard. Heard would later write a definitive history of the legal events that followed the surrender, and he wrote of the release of these hostages. He described "the poor creatures" who "wept for joy at their escape," adding that "[T]he woe written on the faces of these half-starved and nearly naked women and children would have melted the hardest hearts."⁶

Sibley pondered what to do with the captured Indians. For a few days everyone in and around Camp Release went about their business, although the Indians understood they could not flee without being pursued. Sibley finally decided he would appoint a five-member military commission⁷ to find the facts of what had happened. The price to be paid for those found guilty, he decided, would be death by hanging.

Once he made this decision, Sibley quickly had the male Indians chained. There was a significant language barrier, especially concerning such legal matters, but such legal niceties were not destined to detain the proceedings. "Perhaps it will be a stretch of my authority," Sibley wrote of his decision to appoint and empower this commission. "If so, necessity must be my justification."

The language problem was addressed by Sibley in enlisting the services of the Reverend Stephen Riggs, a missionary who had lived in central Minnesota for a few years and spoke the Sioux language well. Riggs tried to communicate to the defendants the legal process, and the seriousness of their position. He then listened and translated their statements for the commission.⁸

Some of the testimony set down by commission secretary Isaac Heard was both eloquent and incriminating. Rdainyanka, or "Rattling Runner," told Riggs that "It was not the intention of the nation to kill any of the whites until the four men returned from Acton and told what they had done. When they did this, all the young men became excited and commenced the massacre. The older ones would have prevented it if they could, but since the treaties they have lost their influence." When discussing what to do as Sibley's army approached them and defeat seemed certain, Rdainyanka counseled the others that "We may regret what has happened, but the matter has gone too far to be remedied. We have got to die. Let us, then, kill as many of the whites as possible, and let the prisoners die with us."[9]

The proceedings conducted by this five-member military commission[10] involved a review of the involvement of some four hundred Indians who were believed to have participated in the attacks. Their exact involvement was the subject of individual, and somewhat hasty fact finding proceedings. The Indian being accused would either plead guilty or profess innocence. Testimony would then be heard from white settlers or soldiers as to the involvement of the particular accused in any attacks. No opportunity to challenge this opposing testimony, no juries, no real deliberation.

The trials of all the accused took six weeks. As facts were found and the list of the accused expanded, the trials quickened in pace. By the end there were often dozens of trials taking place on a single day. In the end, three hundred and three Indians were found guilty and sentenced to be hanged.

II

ANY FAIR ASSESSMENT of the situation in and around Camp Release in October 1862 would have to conclude that a great injustice was being done to the great majority of the Indians there. Apart from the bias involved in the legal proceedings, there were more than a thousand Indians confined to the area, many of them Sisseton and Wahpeton Indians, many more of them women and young children, and the vast majority of them hadn't fought at all.

Recall that President Lincoln, in his address to Congress in July 1861, asserted that the soldiers of the Confederacy were drawn from some states in which secession was not a majority sentiment. President Lincoln was ready and willing to defend with arms and men the interests of those individuals throughout the Confederate states who did not want to secede. President Lincoln wanted to regard the secessionists as insurrectionists.

A majority of the Indians in southern Minnesota, probably one larger than that of the Unionists in any Confederate state, might have been seen by the truly fair-minded as having similar rights worth defending, as being victims of an insurrection within their Indian nation against the same government.

Such fairness, such "charity for all," would not be granted them. Minnesota's political leaders, many of them President Lincoln's political allies, could not muster it. All the Indians would be held and treated as prisoners.

In that same address, President Lincoln had also gone to some trouble to defend his suspension of "habeas corpus," the legal writ that allows those confined by the government without being charged with a crime to challenge that confinement. The president argued the suspension of habeas corpus was a war measure necessary to preserve all the other rights his government still recognized.[11]

No such argument could plausibly apply to these un-charged Indian citizens. The Indians of southern Minnesota in no way threatened the U.S. government's ability to defend the rights and privileges of the citizens of the United States. Yet many Indians remained in government custody after the trials of the warriors were concluded in the fall of 1862. These Indians were, therefore, charged with no crime, yet they were essentially imprisoned. These remaining, mostly innocent Indians, the remnants of a people who had been "once prosperous and happy"—to borrow from the writings of Charles

Flandrau—were then forced to march at the point of a government gun along the Minnesota River.

The plan was to force them on to Fort Snelling, over 120 river miles away.

These innocent Indian prisoners, the majority of them women and children, walked day after day under armed guard as the weather turned cold and the skies of late autumn turned gray, as they do in Minnesota. They had no doubt been told what some of the Indian warriors had done—violent outcasts such as Cut-Nose and Red Middle Voice. In case they forgot for a moment how sure the white settlers were concerning their collective guilt for the crimes committed by others, these Indians were pelted and jeered and threatened along the way.

Surely some of those white settlers who jeered and pelted these Indian prisoners could see that this was simply compounding one injustice with yet another. Some perhaps could, but they were no majority.

The Indians made it to Fort Snelling and set up their camp—surrounded by makeshift walls—along the Minnesota River, in the damp flood plain below the fort. They would spend a cold Minnesota winter there. They were given rations, Civil War soldier's rations, food they did not normally eat. Contagious diseases like measles, diseases to which the Indians had little resistance, spread through the camp. Many would die.[12]

The three hundred Indian warriors who were convicted of participation in the fighting by Sibley's commission were treated far worse, if that's possible. They were chained to one another and placed on wagons that were to take them to Camp Lincoln, near Mankato.

The route they took to Mankato took them near New Ulm.[13] It was mid-November as they neared New Ulm, and many of the refugees who had abandoned New Ulm on August 24th had by mid-November returned home.

Residents of the New Ulm area brutally attacked the prisoners. One of the guards attempting to protect the prisoners recorded that "the citizens were out there, women with their aprons full of brickbats. . . .The first I knew, one very large German woman slipped through in front of me, and hit one of the Indians on the head with a large stone. Well, he fell backwards out of the wagon, he being shackled to another Indian that held him, so he was dragged about five rods [about eighty feet]. Then myself and comrade picked him up and put him back in the wagon."[14]

One of the prisoners, Wakanajaja (later George Crooks), a young man at the time, would later record his fearful memories: "As we came near New Ulm my brother told me the driver was . . . afraid to go through New Ulm, my heart leaped into my mouth, and I crouched down beside my brother completely overcome with fear. In a short time we reached the outskirts of the town and the long looked-for verdict—death—seemed at hand. Women were running about, men waving their arms and shouting at the top of their voices, convinced the driver the citizens of that village were wild for the thirst for blood, so he turned the vehicle in an effort to escape the angry mob but not until . . . they were upon us. We were pounded to a jelly, my arms, feet, and head resembled raw beef steak. How I escaped alive has always been a mystery to me. My brother was killed and when I realized he was dead I felt the only person in the world to look after me was gone and I wished at the time that they had killed me.

"We reached Mankato late that evening . . . I can truthfully say the experience photographed on my youthful mind can never be defaced by time."[15]

III

THE TRIALS OF THE INDIAN WARRIORS were ongoing at Camp Release when they became the subject of a Cabinet meeting in Washington on October 14th. President Lincoln counseled restraint upon his government in Minnesota, but he must have understood it would be difficult for those so close to the calamity to practice it. Lincoln's own General Pope, who never did much of the fighting but was close enough to many white Minnesotans and their views, issued a report to the president. The report was read out loud to the Cabinet that day by Lincoln's Secretary of War Edwin Stanton, and in the report Pope called for "hanging" of hundreds of the warriors.

Lincoln and his Cabinet members were taken aback. Couldn't Pope see this as rash? One of the Cabinet members, long-white-bearded Secretary of the Navy Gideon Welles—a man Lincoln liked to call "Father Neptune"—complained that "I was disgusted with the whole thing. The tone and opinions of the dispatch are discreditable."[16]

What was going on out there in Minnesota?

The difficulty that Minnesotans had in keeping a level head is perhaps best illustrated in the writings of Jane Grey Swisshelm. Swisshelm was a progressive, a firebrand abolitionist and women's rights advocate that Lincoln knew of and perhaps secretly admired. In 1862 she was a St. Cloud, Minnesota, newspaper owner and editor, possessed of a keen eye for spotting and exposing corruption and an acid pen that got her in trouble on occasion.

Jane Grey Swisshelm was a champion of human rights, and before moving to Minnesota from Pennsylvania she was a bit of a romantic regarding the native Americans. ". . . I had the common [James Fenimore] Cooper idea," she wrote, a reference to the author of the popular novel *Last of the Mohicans*, "of the dignity and glory of the noble red man of the forest."[17]

Newspaper owner and editor, Jane Grey Swisshelm.

However, by late August 1862 Swisshelm would have begun to hear and read some of the details of the atrocities committed just 100 miles from St. Cloud. She saw the calamity in progressive terms, and saw the Indians and their behavior as regressive. She criticized Colonel Sibley for not attempting a rescue of the hostages more quickly, and called him "the state undertaker with his company of grave diggers."[18]

As the details rolled in, Swisshelm became virulently anti-Sioux Indian, exhorting her fellow Minnesotans and Civil War veterans to take up their guns and "hunt Sioux. Do not wait to be hunted.

MALICE TOWARD NONE

Exterminate the wild beasts."[19] The details were so contrary to her sense of progress and decency, that she joined the chorus calling for mass executions. She argued that the Indians found guilty of killing the defenseless settlers should be hanged, that there could be no moral ambiguity in such acts. "We cannot breathe the same air with those demon violators of women, crucifiers of infants."

Swisshelm began lecturing on the subject, and she compared the Indians and their government annuity payments with—of all things!—the Southern slaveholders, both of whom she thought "lazy, impudent" types who prospered off the work of others. "The Indian and the Slaveholder have been the aristocrats of American society," she wrote. "Both races must be exterminated or learn the art of working for a living."[20] Whoa!!!

There is no record showing Lincoln read her arguments as they were appearing in print in late 1862, but in 1863 Swisshelm left St. Cloud for a job in Washington, D.C., and was invited to visit the White House to meet the president and Mrs. Lincoln. If President Lincoln did read Swisshelm in late 1862, her remarks about "extermination" were perhaps proof positive for him that cooler heads had to intercede.

It was time for President Lincoln, as leader of the U.S. government, the other party to the Treaties of Traverse des Sioux and Mendota, to step in and exercise the restraint required.

Restraint was indeed required when considering the group of Indians Sibley had captured. By November 1862, the list of prisoners and the list of the convicted had been perused closely. It was becoming uncomfortably clear that many of the known leaders—notably Little Crow—were nowhere on the rolls of the convicted.

President Lincoln sent word through Interior Department channels that nobody was to be hanged just yet, and he demanded the records of the trial proceedings. He asked for "a careful statement" indicating "the more guilty and influential of the culprits."[21] Lincoln's plan was to review these files, along with two Interior Department lawyers, with the sharp eye of a truly gifted lawyer.

The president did not lack for advice from others as he reviewed the files. His agents in Minnesota told him the situation was dire and urgent, and they advised him to approve of a swift justice for those convicted. The trial records were duly sent to Lincoln, along with another note from Major General Pope urging that all the condemned be hanged, and warning of mob violence or vigilantism in Minnesota if they were not. Perhaps because Pope was still held in somewhat low esteem for his loss at the second Bull Run, but probably more because Lincoln considered his own political judgment superior to that of his Army generals, Lincoln ignored Pope's advice.

Bishop Whipple, the Episcopalian leader of the Minnesota diocese, wished to intercede on behalf of the Indians in his home state. He visited Washington, D.C., in mid-September 1862 and stayed at the Georgetown house of Union General Henry Halleck, Whipple's first cousin. Bishop Whipple attempted to arrange a meeting with President Lincoln to discuss the situation in Minnesota. Strangely enough he succeeded, and he was given an interval of time to speak with President Lincoln on September 16th.

Any number of people wanted to speak with the president on the matter of the Civil War and on the matter of the Indians of Minnesota, yet President Lincoln met with the bishop, a quite singular fact that must be analyzed.

Why did Lincoln see Bishop Whipple at all? No other President in American history could be said to have more "on his plate" than did Abraham Lincoln that September of 1862. No man could have so easily claimed to be "too busy" to meet with a clergyman from the sticks.

Perhaps Lincoln had begun to admire the bishop's shrewd political insights. Whipple had written to the president the previous March, months before the attacks, documenting the sad state of affairs with the Indians in Minnesota and the sorry and corrupt state of the president's Indian representatives. We know Lincoln perused this letter, because Lincoln promptly asked the secretary of the Interior to investigate Whipple's assertions. The secretary did so, and proposed reforms.

Whipple understood the effect of the treaties as only one with a real political sense could, and in appealing to President Lincoln he addressed another man with that same political sense. "From the day of the Treaty," he wrote, "a rapid deterioration takes place. The Indian has sold the hunting-grounds necessary for his comfort as a wild man; His tribal relations are weakened; his chief's power and influence circumscribed; and he will soon be left a helpless man without a government, a protector, or a friend, unless treaty is observed."

IT IS EASY TO POINT to aspects of Whipple's mission to the Indians of Minnesota that are not fully acceptable to twenty-first century sensibilities. Whipple preached the Gospel and sought to convert the Indians to Christianity, but he also encouraged adoption of the white man's ways: farming, white man's clothing, even the cutting of hair among the men. Yet Whipple understood the political vacuum created within these tribes when they began living under these treaties alongside the white men, and he understood the injustice it created. Whipple was as good an advocate for the Indians as any other white man within the workings of the white man's world of 1862.

LINCOLN UNDERSTOOD THE SITUATION in Minnesota better than most everyone else in Washington. Lincoln had known something of Indian fighting from serving in the Illinois militia during the Black Hawk War in 1832. Lincoln knew the story of how his own grandfather had been killed by Indians. Lincoln had perhaps requested and read or at least thought more about Whipple's letter sent in March 1862 as he learned more about the events in Minnesota in September and October. Lincoln met with Whipple perhaps because he wanted first-hand information from a man with the demonstrated political reasoning skills Lincoln admired.

The bishop later wrote that the president liked to tell stories, and after Whipple had spoken of the situation in Minnesota, Lincoln made a joke about the number of honest men required to watch over one of the government's Indian agents, a joke that clearly showed he understood the corruption at the heart of the government's dealings with the Indians. When the president was meeting a few days later with a friend from Illinois, Lincoln told him of the extent to which the bishop had opened his eyes. "He [Bishop Whipple] came here the other day and talked with me about the rascality of this Indian business until I felt it down to my boots."[22]

The Battle of Antietam occurred shortly after Bishop Whipple's meeting with President Lincoln, and the bishop left Washington to visit the battlefield. Whipple found and thanked the men of the First Minnesota. At General McClellan's request, he held a religious service at McClellan's camp. The bishop was a well-traveled and world-wise man, but the death and devastation he witnessed in and around the Antietam battlefield would leave a vivid impression upon him.

Whipple proceeded onto New York, where he attended the General Convention of the Episcopal Church that October of 1862. He tried to get many of the other attendees to sign a resolution of sorts that he had drawn up regarding the government's treatment of the Indians. His resolution proposed a commission be appointed by the president to "devise a more perfect system for the administration of Indian affairs."[23] Some of the bishops balked at such political advocacy on the part of the Episcopate—the pastoral letter issued at the close of the Convention was greatly concerned with the effects of the Civil War and contained no mention of the Sioux[24]—but Whipple did get a couple dozen signatures.

Bishop Whipple wrote a letter to the president through Minnesota Senator Henry M. Rice on November 12th in which he put in writing his view that "[W]e cannot hang men by the hundreds . . . We claim that they are an independent nation and as such they are prisoners of war."

Whipple addressed his fellow Minnesotans in an open letter published in some of the state's major newspapers entitled "The Duty of Citizens Concerning the Indian Massacre," admitting that "[T]here is no man who does not feel that the savages who have committed these deeds of violence must meet their doom," but went on to argue for the "strictest scrutiny" in attempting to do justice, making the point that "Punishment loses its lesson when it is the vengeance of a mob."

President Lincoln gave no speeches, and leaked no statements to the press in November 1862 on the issue of what to do with the condemned. Maddeningly silent, as far as Minnesota's political leaders were concerned. Lincoln's annual report was delivered on December 1st, and in it he mentioned that "Minnesota had suffered a great injury from this Indian war," but he did not say what he was going to do about those who were at that moment sentenced to be hanged.

Governor Ramsey announced that "our people have had just reason to complain of the tardiness of executive action." Minnesota Senator Morton Wilkinson introduced a resolution, passed by the Senate on December 5th, demanding the president give a full accounting of his handling of the matter of the condemned Indians.

THE PRESIDENT MADE HIS decisions public on December 6th, in the form of a letter to General Pope. Thirty-nine Indian men were guilty of crimes punishable by death and would be hanged. The rest, the some two hundred and sixty Indians convicted of making war on the settlers and on the U.S. military and sentenced to hang by Sibley's commission, would not be hanged, but instead held by the government as prisoners of war for the time being.

President Lincoln's commutation came too late for the Indian prisoners killed near New Ulm.

President Lincoln had found that almost ninety percent of the Indians convicted by the military commission were perhaps guilty of participation in the warfare, but there was no evidence of malice or cruelty, only evidence that they had behaved as warriors, as soldiers.[25] As such, they would be held as prisoners of war, not as murderers.

The president set forth his reasoning in a letter he drafted in response to the Senate resolution. "I caused a careful examination of the records of trials to be made, in view of first ordering the execution of such as had been proved guilty of violating females," he wrote. "Contrary to my expectations, only two of this class were found. I then directed a further examination, and a classification of all who were proven to have participated in massacres, as distinguished from participation in battles. This class numbered forty, and included the two convicted of female violation. One of the number is strongly recommended, by the commission which tried them, for commutation to ten years' imprisonment. I have ordered the other 39 to be executed on Friday, the nineteenth instant."

President Lincoln had taken Bishop Whipple's advice: it was the violation of settlers, of women and children, that was in no way consistent with a declaration of war, and where true culpability for murder should lie.

Lincoln knew that his exhortation to the Cooper Union audience those many months earlier that they should have faith that "Right makes Might" was the exception to the time-honored rule among men that "Might makes Right." What the Indians attempted in Minnesota— wresting back their land when they believed the treaty terms had been broken—was an invocation of the old, time-honored rule and a routine act of war, not malicious murder. It was only those who were cruel to the defenseless, Lincoln ruled, who were truly guilty of a capital crime.

Cut-Nose had claimed little involvement in the war initially when questioned during his trial, saying he only joined in the fighting with the others. The evidence against him provided by others, however, was considerable. He was sentenced to be hanged, and once sentenced he boasted of having killed some twenty-seven whites. Whatever the number, he probably counted among his victims Catherine and Johan and Sarah Kochendorfer.[26]

His case went to Washington for review by President Lincoln along with the others. The president's search for evidence that Cut-Nose had participated in massacres would have been availing. Cut-Nose, "Mehpo-o-ko-na-ji" in Lincoln's own handwriting, convicted prisoner number 96 by the court's recording system, was sentenced by President Lincoln to hang.

Evidence was found that exonerated one of the thirty-nine Indians, but the remaining thirty-eight were marched onto a scaffold in central Mankato on the day after Christmas 1862. Some five thousand people looked on as three slow drum beats sounded. On the third beat

William Duley, the father of two victims, came forward and cut the rope that caused the platform beneath each of the condemned to fall. It was, and remains today, the largest mass execution in American history. One of the thirty eight ropes is said to have broken—the rope surrounding the neck of either Rdinyanka or Cut-Nose, accounts vary—and although Isaac Heard records that the body appeared lifeless on the ground, it was hastily re-hung along with the others.

There was some medical interest in the skeletal remains of these Indians. To the white man's sensibilities, these Indians were not deserving of any reverent, religious burial. The bodies were surreptitiously taken from their graves and allowed to freeze in the December cold, and they were then sold as cadavers. The remains of Cut-Nose were claimed by Dr. William Mayo, one of the doctors who had rushed from Le Sueur to New Ulm when the city was attacked in August. Dr. Mayo cleaned and kept the skeletal remains of Cut-Nose for study and illustration; indeed he passed them down to his sons, William and Charles Mayo, who would study them as well.[27] His sons, the founders of the world-famous Mayo Clinic in Rochester, Minnesota, kept the skeleton of Cut-Nose for many years, displaying the skeletal remains for illustration and as a curiosity for those who knew the story of the events of 1862.

The year 1862 was calamitous for Minnesotans, but it was also a dreadful year for the country at large. The Second Battle of Bull Run in late-August was followed by the terrible Battle of Antietam in mid-September, during which over twenty-six thousand soldiers were killed, wounded, or unaccounted for. There was precious little concern throughout the rest of the country for the few dozen Indian deaths that December 1862 in Mankato, or indeed for the many other Indian deaths that followed during their imprisonment.

The first day of 1863 offered hope, though. The provisions of the Emancipation Proclamation were triggered in the Confederate-held territories, and the slaves there were suddenly free men in the eyes of the federal government. On that same first day of January 1863, federal land offices began filing land claims under the provisions of the Homestead Act of 1862. Over four hundred claims would be filed that first day.

In practical terms, however, the year 1863 would not see things get much better. The Civil War raged on, hatreds deepened, welling up to the climactic Battle of Gettysburg in early July. Amid all the bloodshed, the Union lines held their ground, and the tide finally turned for good in favor of the Union. Lincoln's Union, with its superior munitions and its seemingly inexhaustible supply of soldiers and generals, would now prevail. It was only a matter of time and lives.

Lincoln and the Republicans had concerns over the approaching election of 1864 during the winter and spring of that year, but the decisive Union victories in the late summer of 1864 in north Georgia put the issue to rest. Lincoln would win re-election easily, even more decisively than in 1860.

Minnesotans were still in the Lincoln camp in November 1864, but not so solidly as before. Indeed, most of the Union states voted somewhat more strongly for Lincoln in 1864 than in 1860—but Minnesota did not. Lincoln got fifty-nine percent of the Minnesota vote in 1864 in a two-man race with former General George McClellan, the same man he had promoted and then dismissed two years earlier. This fifty-nine percent of the vote was enough to win Minnesota's electoral votes, but it was down from his overwhelming 63.4 percent of the vote in the four-man race in 1860. Lincoln's margin of victory in Minnesota in 1864, while still wide, was only roughly half what it had been in 1860.

Alexander Ramsey had been appointed to the Senate from Minnesota by 1864, and he had occasion to discuss the 1864 election results in his home state with his fellow Republican politician, Abraham Lincoln. Ramsey records in his diary that the president, on addressing Ramsey, was a little miffed at the decline in his margin of victory in Minnesota.

"If you'd have hung more Indians, we would have given you your old majority," Ramsey records he told the president.

"I could not afford to hang men for votes," President Lincoln told him.[28]

Notes

[1] Carley, pp. 41-44.

[2] Letter from General Pope to General in Chief Henry W. Halleck, posted from St. Paul on September 30, 1862. It is an interesting historical fact that General-in-Chief Halleck was Bishop Henry Whipple's cousin, a fact that perhaps improved Bishop Whipple's access to President Lincoln and other Washington power-brokers.

[3] Oehler, p. 192. The author suggests the trek to the Yellow Medicine River could have been accomplished in a day.

[4] *Through Dakota Eyes*—Thomas A. Robertson's narrative 2. Thomas Roberston, a twenty-two-year old "half-breed," served as a go-between for Little Crow and Colonel Sibley. He was present near Camp Release, where his mother, brothers, and a sister were held captive. He recalls that the Indians "decided to attack the camp that night or early in the morning, and everybody was ordered to go that night. As usually supposed, these orders were not from Little Crow but by the Soldiers' Lodge, of whom the notorious Cut-Nose . . . was the head, and who was virtually in command at all the battles."

[5] Oehler, p. 206.

[6] *History of the Sioux War* by Isaac V.D. Heard (1864), p. 186.

[7] The Indians were not members of the armed forces and, therefore, not subject to military law, so the proceedings were sometimes mislabeled a "courts-martial." The law governing the legal proceedings, the precise combination of military and civil law, was not defined.

[8] Recorder Isaac Heard wrote that Riggs was "in effect, the Grand Jury of the court. His long residence in the country, and extensive acquaintance with the Indians, his knowledge of the character and habits of most of them, enabling him to tell almost with certainty what Indians would be implicated and what ones not." Heard, p. 251.

[9] *History of the Sioux War* by I.V.D. Heard (1864), pp. 151-152.

[10] Oehler, p. 203. All were soldiers under Sibley's command. All had only recently finished fighting the Sioux being tried. The acting judge, Lieutenant Olin, had also just finished fighting the Sioux.

[11] President Lincoln put it this way in his July 5, 1861, message to Congress: "To state the question more directly, are all the laws, but one, to go unexecuted, and the government itself go to pieces, lest that one be violated?"

[12] "There were a considerable number of deaths in the camp after the list was made out." This was the laconic assessment of Assistant Adjutant General R.C. Olin in a letter dated May 26,1863. Olin was tasked in December 1862 with making a list of the Indians *"under the surveillance"* of the U.S. military at Fort Snelling that winter. The italics used above were those of General Olin, a vain attempt at convincing posterity that the Indians camped at Fort Snelling were merely being monitored and not being imprisoned without charge.

[13] There are, of course, other routes they could have taken to get to Mankato.

[14]*Reminiscences of the Sioux Outbreak*, A.B. Watson. Dakota Conflict of 1862. Minnesota Historical Society, Manuscripts Collections.

[15]*Morton Enterprise*, January 29, 1909. The town of Morton is on the opposite side and just downstream of Redwood Falls. *The Redwood Gazette* later re-printed the story, and someone identifying himself as George Crooks phoned the *Gazette* to deny this account, saying that his older brother did not die at New Ulm but survived the trip to Mankato and imprisonment. Whatever the case, various sources have fifteen Indians severely injured and/or "a few" prisoners dying from the beatings they suffered that day near New Ulm.

[16]*Diary of Gideon Welles*, Volume I, p. 171. Welles, a shrewd Connecticut Yankee, deplored Pope's warlike stance, writing that there were undoubtedly outrages, "but what may have been the provocation we are not told."

[17]*Half a Century* by J. Grey Swisheim (1881), p. 223

[18]*St. Cloud Democrat*, August 1862.

[19]*St. Cloud Democrat*, Sept 4, 1862.

[20]*Half a Century* by J. Grey Swisshelm, pp. 223-228.

[21]*Minnesota in the Civil and Indian Wars*, *St. Paul Pioneer Press* (1890) - Letter of President Lincoln to General Pope.

[22]Cox, p. 165.

[23]Cox, p. 164.

[24]*Pastoral Letter of the Bishops of the Protestant Episcopal Church in the United States of America*, delivered before the General Convention, October 17, 1862: ". . . We look in vain for the occupants of seats in the Convention, belonging to the representative of no less than ten of our Dioceses, and to ten of our Bishops."

[25]*History of Minnesota* by W. Folwell (1924). Lincoln had charged Interior Department lawyers George Whiting and Francis Ruggles with the task of distinguishing between those guilty of crimes and those guilty only of participation in battles.

[26]*Through Dakota Eyes*, edited by G.C. Anderson and A.R. Woolworth (1988) Samuel J. Brown, a seventeen-year-old, was captured by Cut-Nose and his band near Middle Creek on Tuesday, August 19th, and spared because of his "half-breed" status. Brown described Cut-Nose as the "ugliest looking and most repulsive specimen of humanity that I had ever seen," p. 77. Four weeks later, a prisoner at Camp Release, Brown watched the warriors dance and boast of their warring exploits. One of the boasting Lower Sioux was a "hideous looking fellow" who claimed he "had dispatched three—a man, a woman, and a child—and then proceed[ed] to act out the sufferings of his victims." p. 174. The man was dispatched by being shot in the back. The editors believe the family so dispatched was the Kochendorfers, p.216, footnote 6. The "hideous looking fellow" was probably Cut-Nose.

[27]Carley, p. 75.

[28]Alexander Ramsey Diary, November 23, 1864.

"Who Shall Have Borne the Battle"

I

The events of the early 1860s can be analyzed any number of ways: the grand sweep of history, the political, the economic, etc. We have looked at that grand sweep, but our real focus has been on particular people caught up in that grand sweep, and our inquiry will now turn to how they allowed these events to affect them. Some permitted their hatred and their warring spirit to poison, and then often shorten, their lives. Others were left with an empty feeling that they should have known and done something more when things were reaching such a dreadful pass. Still others did their best to reconcile themselves and others to what had happened.

The warriors who fled the area near Camp Release went north and west, into Dakota and Chippewa country.

Leader Little Crow spent the ensuing winter in the Dakota country and in Canada with his women and children and braves. He tried to rally other tribes to his banner and attack the white settlers, but with little success. It is interesting to consider how this leader, initially reluctant to declare war, allowed the act of warfare to create in him an antipathy towards the white settlers and the government that perhaps did not exist before the fighting started.

Little Crow felt he needed more horses to lead his tribe further west and there to continue his battle against General Pope's forces. He could not resist the pull of his home lands in Minnesota, however. He knew farmers there who had plenty of horses, and near present day Hutchinson, as he and one of his sons were eating berries right off some bushes, he was shot dead by a farmer, and his body was thrown on a garbage heap nearby.[1]

Red Middle Voice fled north, into Chippewa country, and as the teaching goes concerning those who "live by the sword," he perished in a battle with the Chippewa.[2]

Most of the Indians who survived the march to Fort Snelling and the winter there were sent by steamboat down the Mississippi in May 1863. The first of two steamboats, filled with hundreds of Indians guarded by U.S. soldiers, stopped at the St. Paul landing. The Indians on board were pelted with stones thrown by an angry mob that had gathered near the landing, a mob that was only dispersed when the soldiers threatened the mob with bayonets.[3] The steamboats were headed south and then up the Missouri River, into the Dakota Territory, to a wind-swept spot on the prairie along the Missouri River near present-day Chamberlain, South Dakota. The prairie there proved unsuitable for farming, and many were allowed to move back down the Missouri River, onto a reservation just south of the river, in Nebraska.

August Busse was fourteen years old on August 18th of 1862, working on his family farm near Middle Creek, when he was sent on an errand to the Roessler farm nearby. On arriving at the Roessler's he found all of them killed, and on returning to his family's farm he discovered that both his parents and his two sisters had been shot and killed while fleeing. August Busse ended up a prisoner at Camp Release, and he left the camp determined to exact his revenge upon the Indians. He moved to Montana, joined the army, and eventually found himself under the command of Lieutenant Colonel George Armstrong Custer.[4]

As mentioned earlier, only two of the nine people who lived at the Schwandt farm near Middle Creek survived. Mary was working at the Reynolds' store, away from her parents' farm, and she was taken prisoner and survived to be rescued by Sibley's men at Camp Release. She and her brother August Schwandt were reunited months later at a relative's farm in Wisconsin. Neither had been told that the other had survived, and although they were happy to be reunited, the tremendous weight of their loss was difficult for them.

They did try their best to forget. "The memory of that period, with all its hideous features, comes before me," Mary wrote in 1894 at the request of the Minnesota Historical Society, "but I put it down." She wrote philosophically that "I have seen much of the agreeable side of life, too." She married and had children, and for many years she lived near her brother in Portland, Oregon, before returning with her husband to live in Minnesota, in St. Paul.

Mary Schwandt's memories of her captivity included an encounter with Little Crow that she committed to paper. "I was sitting quietly by a tepee when he came along dressed in full chief's costume and looking very grand," she wrote. "Suddenly he jerked his tomahawk from his belt and sprang toward me with the weapon uplifted as if he meant to cleave my head in two. I remember, as well as if it were only an hour ago. Then he glared down upon me so savagely, that I thought he would kill me; but I looked up at him without any fear or care about my fate, and gazed quietly into his face without so much as winking my tear-swollen eyes. He brandished the tomahawk over me a few times, then laughed, put it back in his belt, still laughing and saying something in Indian. . . . Some people say he had many noble traits of character, but I have another opinion of any man, savage or civilized, who will scare, for a subject of sport a poor, weak, defenseless, broken girl, a prisoner in his hands."[5]

Mary survived to tell her story largely due to the protection given her during her captivity by an Indian woman named Snana (later Maggie Brass). Snana grew up on the Kaposia lands near St. Paul, and she learned English at a missionary school there before marrying and moving to the reservation along the Minnesota River. Snana had three children of her own in 1862, but her oldest child died shortly before the Uprising began, and she missed her very much and wanted to replace her with another daughter. Snana traded a pony to the warriors to obtain Mary, then bravely guarded her, and on at least one occasion concealed Mary from her torturers.[6] Snana turned Mary Schwandt over to the soldiers at Camp Release, writing later of losing Mary that "my heart ached again; but afterward I knew that I had done something which was right."[7]

Snana would suffer along with many other innocent Indians present at Camp Release in September 1862. She made the long walk to Fort Snelling, along with her husband and their two young children. Her two children, like so many others, did not survive the winter of 1862-1863 at Fort Snelling. Her husband left her to join Henry Sibley's forces in pursuit of Little Crow and his warriors, serving as a scout. Now alone, Snana lived a few years near Faribault, Minnesota, before moving south to the reservation in Nebraska to live with other tribe members alongside the Santee Indians. She married a second time there, and adopted two children.

Snana and Mary Schwandt together in St. Paul, 1899.

Years later, Mary Schwandt sought Snana out. "I want you to know," Mary wrote, "that the little captive German girl you so often befriended and shielded from harm loves you still for your kindness and care." In 1894, Snana's second husband died and she traveled to St. Paul to see Mary Schwandt again, writing that she was treated there "just as if I went to visit my own child."[8] The two of them—proud survivors—were photographed together at about that time.

In the months and years following those calamitous events in 1862, the advantage of hindsight made certain writings and events appear morbidly clairvoyant. Catherine Kochendorfer wrote a letter to a preacher friend back in Illinois in the weeks before her death in which she seemed resigned to her own impending death. "Not barring what the future will bring," she wrote, "and this should be my last writing to you. I only hope we'll have a get together in eternity. I am unaware how soon the end will be for me, but I have one foot in the grave already. I am still needed and wanted by my family and God alone knows when He'll take me away from here into His own house." Following the events of August 18th, that particular passage seemed mysteriously prescient to all who read it.

Mary Schwandt recalled her family's arrival in the river valley that spring of 1862, and their first encounter with the Indians. "My sister, Mrs. Walz, was much frightened at them. She cried and sobbed in her terror, and even hid herself in the wagon and would not look at them, so distressed was she. I have often wondered whether she did not then have a premonition of the dreadful fate she was destined to suffer."[9]

Margaret King Hern had more tangible premonitions. She later wrote that "Three weeks before the outbreak, the Sioux Indians had a war dance back of the fort and claimed it was against the Chippewas. At first we believed them, but when the half breed, Indian Charlie, came in to borrow cooking utensils, he sat down and hung his head, as if under the influence of liquor. He kept saying 'Too bad! Too bad!'

"Mrs. Dunn [another soldier's wife] became suspicious and knowing I knew him well, as he had often stopped at our cabin, said 'Ask him what is too bad.' He said, 'Injuns kill white folks. Me like white folks. Me like Injuns. Me have to fight. Me don't want to.' He seemed to feel broken-hearted. I did not believe him and thought him drunk, but Mrs. Dunn said, 'You go over and tell [ordnance officer] Sergeant [John] Jones what he said.' I did. Sergeant Jones said, 'What nonsense! They are only going to have their war dance.'"[10]

Women certainly are more given to indulging, remembering, and recording their feelings than men, but they are also more sensitive to potential problems that may prevail in certain social situations. Is it possible that these women could sense friction between the whites and the Indians the men could not? It is distinctly possible.

Margaret King Hern would return to civilian life following the events of the early 1860s, but she would never forget those days at Fort Ridgely. The State of Minnesota would never forget her service there, either. In 1896, the State dedicated a monument at Fort Ridgely to "commemorate the heroism of the soldiers and the citizens . . . who successfully defended the Fort." Margaret King Hern was presented with a medal by the State, a medal inscribed with her name and identifying her as a "Defender of Fort Ridgely."

The nearby town of New Ulm was nearly destroyed by the events of 1862, but it recovered. The citizens were angry about the Indian attacks, but they were proud of the defense they had managed. The city leaders of New Ulm have always been proud of their German heritage as well, and in 1888 they commissioned a monument and statue to commemorate this heritage. "Hermann the German," a copper-and-iron figure from Germany's semi-mythical past, now stands proudly above a circular colonnade and thrusts a sword proudly into the air. From his spot one hundred feet above the ground, Hermann the German looks out over the Minnesota River Valley

The Hermann Monument, New Ulm, Minnesota. (Courtesy of Allan R. Gebhard)

and over what had been reservation land in 1862. Hermann—"Arminius" in Latin—was a German tribal leader who in the year 9 A.D. was credited with leading his fellow tribesmen in an ambush of three Roman legions in the Battle of Teutoburg Forest, Romans who believed they were extending civilization and the benefits of "Pax Romana" to the more primitive people of Germania. New Ulm's civic leaders dedicated the finished work in 1897. Did any of them see irony in dedicating a monument to such a figure, one whose actions might easily be seen as little different from those of Little Crow thirty-five years before?

PRESIDENT LINCOLN'S UNION finally won the war with the Confederacy. Ever the shrewd politician, Lincoln knew that reconciliation would be difficult, but that it had to begin as soon as possible. He did his best to diffuse the hatreds built up during the fighting, but he perhaps knew that he himself could not fully succeed.

On being inaugurated president a second time in March 1865, with fighting still going on just a few dozen miles away, he gave voice to this hope that the sides could be reconciled. "With malice toward none, with charity for all," he said in concluding his speech from the lectern perched above a rain-soaked Capitol grounds, "with firmness in the right as God gives us to see the right, let us strive on to finish the work we are in, to bind up the nation's wounds, to care for him who shall have borne the battle and for his widow and his orphan, to do all which may achieve and cherish a just and lasting peace among ourselves and with all nations."

President Lincoln might as well have been speaking of the peace he hoped to achieve with the Indians of Minnesota as well as with the states of the South. We will never know the full measure of his ability to heal and reconcile the warring sides. A few weeks later and just days after the Confederacy's official surrender, Abraham Lincoln was shot dead at Ford's Theatre in Washington, D.C., by a rabid Confederate sympathizer, who was himself then hunted down and shot and his four co-conspirators summarily hanged.

Bishop Henry Whipple, Lincoln's guide to the situation in Minnesota, continued his mission work, and he continued to try to convert the Indians and to champion their humane treatment. The

Indians returned his concern for them by referring to him as "Straight Tongue," a measure of their respect for his honesty and his good intentions. Bishop Whipple was at his religious core a "High Church" man, a nineteenth-century Episcopalian, but his diocese was in the rugged west, and he reconciled these two facts by being tolerant for all who truly believed in or who wished to learn the essential teachings of Christ, and of the crucifixion, and the resurrection.

Bishop Whipple never held any official government position, yet one of the larger and more prominent federal buildings in Minnesota is named after him. The Bishop Henry Whipple Federal Building sits a mile or so from Fort Snelling, near the bluffs overlooking the Minnesota River, and near the edge of the Minneapolis-St. Paul International Airport. The Whipple Building looks out over and across the river valley down at the Sibley House on the opposite side, the stone mansion Henry Sibley built with the money he made trading with the Indians. These two different buildings, associated with these two very different men, who dealt with the Indians of Minnesota in such different ways, now face each other implacably from either side of the mouth of the Minnesota River.

Henry Sibley and Alexander Ramsey, Minnesota's early political leaders, who worked so closely with the Fillmore, Buchanan, and then Lincoln administrations in the 1850s and 1860s, continued in political life into the 1880s. Their political prominence and their importance, however, would never be the same as it was in those early years.

Henry Sibley, the frontiersman and Indian trader and first governor of the state, may have felt a certain responsibility for the terrible events of 1862, and he spent years leading military expeditions to the western edge of the state to drive the Indians out of the state and into the Dakota Territory. Sibley died in 1891.

Alexander Ramsey, always a healthy and vigorous fellow, lived into the twentieth century, to the ripe old age of eighty-eight. In his later years, he must have looked about him at the tremendous material progress of his state and of the city of St. Paul, at the garish mansions being built up on the hill overlooking the city on Summit Avenue, and he might possibly have contrasted it with the primitive situation that had prevailed just fifty years before, when he negotiated the Treaty of Traverse des Sioux beneath that canopy of tree boughs near St. Peter.

Jane Grey Swisshelm left St. Cloud and Minnesota in late 1862 to work in Washington, D.C., as a clerk—one of the first female clerks—in the quartermaster general's office. She also served as a nurse in aid of the Union Army. Her care for wounded Union soldiers probably did nothing to reduce her antipathy for the Southern slaveholders, and she allowed that antipathy to get the better of her. Following the war, she began another newspaper, *Reconstructionist*, where her views against slavery and slaveholders led her to argue for harsh treatment of the southern states. President Andrew Johnson was the architect of the U.S. government's reconstruction policy, and he was not amused by Swisshelm's views. She lost her government job, and later she shut down her newspaper when the press room and her nearby living apartment were attacked by an arsonist.

The South had surrendered to end the Civil War, but there would be no such quick surrender by the Indians. The Indians of the central Missouri River valley were no less ready to defend their lands than those of southern Minnesota, perhaps having been encouraged to do so by those who had been driven out of Minnesota by Colonel Sibley's and General Pope's forces.

Their great victory would be at the Little Big Horn, in Montana, in 1876. Dakotah and Cheyenne tribes combined there, and among them there were at least a few warriors who had fled Camp Release fourteen years before. They drew in, surrounded and killed all of the two hundred or so United States soldiers under the command of Lieutenant-Colonel George Custer as well as Custer himself. Among the casualties was believed to be one August Busse, who those same fourteen years before had been a prisoner at Camp Release and who had vowed to take revenge upon the Indians.[11]

II

WE MUST RETURN TO the Kochendorfers, though, those four brave young survivors, now orphans, who made it to Fort Ridgely, who helped with the defense of the fort against the two attacks, and who then made it to St. Paul and to safety in September 1862, for it is their story that really needs telling.

Johan, Rosina, Catherine, and Margaret had boarded the steamboat *New Ulm* bound for St. Paul, but en route downstream the boat hit a log or a snag and sank. "The upper deck was not submerged," Rosina remembered, "and there the crew managed to distribute the passengers so that the boat kept on its keel until all persons on board had gone ashore in skiffs."

The children eventually made it to St. Paul, with nothing but the clothes on their back, probably the same clothes they had been wearing on August 18th. The city was in an uproar concerning the Indians and the Civil War, but citizens were also concerned for the white settlers pouring into town.

Governor Ramsey's daughter later wrote that "these poor victims had seen their houses burned and their nearest and dearest tortured and killed before their eyes. There were instances of little boys ten or eleven years old who carried a baby sister or brother all the way to St. Paul . . . . There was no other thought but to help these poor people."[12]

She might as well have been writing specifically about the Kochendorfer children.

Once in St. Paul, however, these four young orphans were among concerned friends, and especially the members of the St. Paul Evangelical Church. News of the death of their fellow church members appeared in the *St. Paul Evangelical Church Bulletin* that September:

Johan Kochendorfer born in Wuerttemberg in 1826,[13] came to America 12 or 13 years ago, settled near Peoria, Ill., there attended the Evangelical Church, where he was converted. In the summer of 1857 he with his family drove in a covered wagon to Prairie du Chien, Wis. There they boarded a steamboat went to St. Paul, where they lived till April 1862, then went on their claim near Beaver Creek, where he was killed in the Indian Massacre Aug. 18, 1862. This dear Brother was highly esteemed among Church friends as well as outsiders. He was a true Christian, and during his Christian life served as Classleader and other work in the Church. His talk was "yes" and "no." At his death he was 36 years old. With him, his wife

Maria Kathryn Lechler Kochendorfer, born in 1826 too, lost her life at the same time. She too was born in Wuerttemberg, Germany, was married soon after coming to this country. She also was a consecrated Christian. Several days before her death she wrote to a friend that "we never know how soon the call may come for us to leave this world." She was ready to follow her Lord's call. Her youngest daughter, Sarah, three years old, was also killed. Four children, Johan 11, Rosina 9, Katherine 7, and Margaret 5, escaped to mourn the death of their loved ones. May God guide and lead them.[14]

The children spent the first weeks with the Feldhouser family, fellow church members who had been close to their parents. Shortly after, little Margaret was sent to live with the Reverend and Mrs. Von Wald of the Evangelical Association, while the three older children went across the Mississippi to stay with Gottfried and Mary Schmidt, the same Schmidts who had been founding members along with the Kochendorfers of the Trinity Evangelical Church of St. Paul. The Schmidts farmed land just on the other side of the Mississippi from the city, and in this calamity they saw what they must do. All four children stayed with the Schmidts for some time that fall.

The children made a trip by steamer to St. Louis late that fall, perhaps to meet with their aunt and uncle from Woodford County, but they returned to St. Paul the following spring, perhaps because their aunt and uncle simply could not afford to care for them all in addition to their own children.[15]

Their church community in St. Paul had by then been given a little time to consider how to care for the four Kochendorfer children, and they had a plan. It wasn't going to be easy, though: the four children were going to have to be split up.

Johan would stay on with the Schmidts. Margaret would stay with Minister Von Wald and his family for a few months, but she would then move in with the Schmidts as well. Their church had made contact with other churches nearby, and members of those congregations also saw a duty in this calamity. Rosina would move across the St. Croix, to western Wisconsin, and stay and help work on the Keller farm, in Trimbelle Township, just east of the mouth of the St. Croix

River. Catherine would move about twenty miles south of St. Paul, to live with members of the Emmanuel Evangelical Church there, the Muellers, who farmed near Hampton, Minnesota.

The little family of seven that had gotten off the steamboat with their horses and their milk cow and had lunched along the Minnesota River's edge the year before was no more. The force of events had thrown them all to the wind.

The Schmidts were truly life-savers for these children, in ways that transcended mere material support. Gottfried and Mary had taken in and adopted an eighteen-month old Mdewakanton Sioux Indian boy in 1854 (at the Indian father's request) and were raising him to adulthood, teaching him German and English, taking him to church, and giving him a new name—Charles—as well as their family name. "Charley" Schmidt was about the same age as young Johan Kochendorfer, and the two of them worked the farm together with the Schmidts. Johan might have felt some hatred for the Indians who had killed his parents, but how could he not see his fellow adopted brother had nothing to do with those events?[16] The Schmidts and their charity—in both word and deed— worked to heal the young Kochendorfers, perhaps Johan especially, in a way that with the advantage of the years seems almost too good to be true.

There is a photograph of Johan and Charles taken about 1870, when both were around eighteen years of age. They both look proudly at the camera. Their skin color is quite different, but they look upon that cameraman as brothers.

While so many others touched by the events of 1862 were letting those events ruin some part of the rest of their lives, Johan and

John Kochendorfer and Charles Schmidt, the adopted sons of Gottfried and Mary Schmidt. (Courtesy of Marilyn Hoffman)

Margaret were growing up alongside young Charley (Margaret called him "Charley" in some of her writings) Schmidt, and learning not to hate.

The Biblical guidance to "lay aside every weight"[17] is a struggle for most of its followers. We are all saddled with difficulties, and laying them aside and looking past them is not easy. The story of these four Kochendorfer orphans is one wherein some may find a source of strength. A much heavier burden than that borne by those four children is hard to imagine, yet they were able to lay it aside, and to "run with perseverance the race that is set before us." They were able to look instead to their remaining blessings, with the help of their new families and their neighbors and their friends.

At the same moment when Jane Grey Swisshelm was living in Washington, D.C., and making sulfurous speeches about "extermination" of "wild beasts," Johan Kochendorfer—a true victim of the attacks, one who had watched his defenseless father and mother and little sister killed—was waking up early to do chores and later looking up at the stars in the night sky alongside his brother Charley.

The four Kochendorfers who survived the attacks of August 1862 lived for many years afterwards, were quoted in newspapers, and Johan and Margaret committed their recollections of the events to paper, yet none of these recordings suggests any hatred of or any general ill-will towards the Indian people. Their parents Johan and Catherine, then Gottfried and Mary Schmidt and their other adoptive parents had taught their children well. They could have blamed their lot in life on a cruel world, or on the Indians, or perhaps later in life on the government—but they didn't. In modern parlance they "got past it," and in doing so they thrived.

The children must have felt very much at home on these farms. Johan continued to work the Schmidt farm until he married Philopena Bach of nearby Woodbury, Minnesota. They were married in 1877, and Johan took up farming his own land very near where he had farmed with the Schmidts.

Rosina was the first of the four children to marry. She was only sixteen when she married Theodore Keller in 1869, one of the sons of Thomas Keller who had taken her in. Theodore had become a widower in 1865, and Theodore and Rosina continued to live and work the farm near Trimbelle Township.

Catherine married Jacob Stapf of Farmington in 1872, and the two of them also took up farming in the area.

Margaret lived with the Schmidts until she married John Erchinger in 1882. She and John moved across the river to live in the city of St. Paul.

Just as they were for August Busse, the events of 1862 were difficult for Johan Kochendorfer to completely forget, but not because of any pent-up hatred. His heart was looking for closure, perhaps some final reconciliation.

Johan made a few trips back to the farm in Flora Township during the 1870s and 1880s. He made the acquaintance of Henry Timms, the man who in 1866 had begun farming what had been the Kochendorfer land. Johan explained to Mr. Timms his connection to the land. Johan knew his parents had been given a hasty burial, and that the cabin he had built with his father and that might have helped him narrow his search had been burned down. A look about the property showed nothing that could be construed as a grave marker. As was mentioned, the burial detail sent out from Fort Ridgely two weeks after their deaths had plenty of bodies to bury and a good deal of incentive to want to get the work done quickly and get back to the fort. Johan returned to St. Paul, perhaps disappointed at not having put more finality to the events of 1862.

The Kochendorfers were well done with what they had seen of the frontier, and of the Indian wars. The state of Minnesota was similarly done: the Indians were moved off their reservation along the Minnesota River, and Fort Ridgely was closed in 1867, there being no more treaty terms left to enforce.

What had happened in Bessarabia fifty years before by czarist order—driving hunting and gathering people off fertile land to make room for farmers—had happened in fits and starts in democratic Minnesota. The czar's absolute power allowed for one swift act of injustice, but no stability. The Bessarabian Germans did not "integrate" their ways with those of their neighbors, and later they would be deported. The Minnesota experience was also unjust, and much more difficult in those formative years, but its institutions would slowly, inexorably, force Minnesotans to integrate their ways—in a manner that the czar's orders never could.

The process would be slow, however. While the Kochendorfer children were growing to adulthood and starting families, the wars between the various Indian tribes and the United States military droned on further west. Braves grew to adulthood hearing stories of the unfair treatment they had received from, and how they had been cheated by, the U.S. government. The U.S. government, for its part, recalled the ambushes and sent its forces out to the frontier to continue to hunt down suspected tribes. Skirmishes occurred all along the frontier.

The events at Little Big Horn were a rallying cry for the Indians, but they were also the last straw for the U.S. government. With each year, the wealth and power of the U.S. government increased, and with it that same government's increased insistence on getting its way, and in keeping a firm peace within its borders.

The arc of history that collided with the Indians of the Great Plains in the nineteenth century is a truly tragic story. When those tribes living along the Missouri River confronted the U.S. government for the first time in the fall of 1804 in the persons of U.S. Army Captains Meriwether Lewis and William Clark and their odd sailboats, they could have had no idea of the developing force these white men represented. These Indians were staunch defenders of their right to their glorious lands and its abundant, sustaining wildlife. They would not surrender their ways without a fight, but the U.S. government was a force so strong it was destined to remake the continent, and later the entire world.

The final, climactic battle between the plains Indians and the U.S. military occurred at Wounded Knee, in South Dakota, in 1890. It wasn't really a battle. Government officials had simply become nervous concerning the spiritual dances being done with more frequency on the Indian lands, and they decided to arrest tribal leader Sitting Bull to quell what they saw as a craze or a cult ritual, or worse, a war dance. Sitting Bull resisted arrest, and in the melee Sitting Bull, seven other Indians, and six U.S. officials were killed.

U.S. officials then decided the entire tribe should be disarmed, and they surrounded Chief Big Foot's band and escorted them to Wounded Knee Creek, on the Pine Ridge Reservation in South Dakota. The following morning the government officials attempted to disarm them, but the inevitable scuffle resulted in nervous officials opening fire and killing or severely wounding most of the tribe of some three hundred. Thirty or so government officials were also killed, some perhaps from shots fired by other officials. It was all so needlessly violent and unfair.

Tribal leader American Horse testified concerning these events to the commissioner of Indian Affairs in February 1891, and complained of the killing of women and children. "[I]t would have been all right," he said, "if only the men were killed; we would feel almost grateful for it. But the fact of the killing of the women, and more especially the killing of the young boys and girls who are to go to make up the future strength of the Indian people, is the saddest part of the whole affair and we feel it very sorely."[18]

A FEW MONTHS LATER, in the late spring of 1891, Henry Timms was digging a new set of fence posts on his land near Middle Creek in Flora Township when he came across the remains of a man, a woman, and a young child. He knew what to do. He wrote Johan Kochendorfer back in St. Paul, and Johan claimed the remains as those of his parents and younger sister.

Johan brought the remains back to St. Paul, the place he thought of as his home, as well as perhaps the real home of his family. The Kochendorfer family had lived happily in St. Paul from 1857 until their move to Flora Township in 1862, and Johan perhaps wanted to remember those years, those happy years, when they were all together.

The South St. Paul newspaper carried the news of Johan's return from Flora Township early that July, his plans, and a brief story of how his family members had died.

Johan arranged for a burial, a re-interment, for the 8th of July 1891, in Oakland Cemetery.

Things had changed substantially for Johan and his three sisters by July 1891. They were now all married and had children of their own and were well-established members of their communities. Johan was now forty years old, and he had three sons: Milton, Alfred, and Karl. Rosina, in Wisconsin, had six children: Charles, Perley, Edna, Zenia, Flsig, and Erma. Margaret, living close by in St. Paul, had three children: Raymond, Cora, and Olive. Catherine in Farmington had fully eight children: John, Anna Marie, Emmanuel, Emily, Jacob, Walter, Martin, and Albert.

All together, the siblings, children, and grandchildren of the three family members being re-interred that day would have numbered twenty four.

It is not known exactly how many of them made it to Oakland Cemetery for the formal burial that July day in 1891. Rosina might have had a little trouble getting her family to St. Paul from Trimbelle Township as it would have involved a thirty mile journey and crossing the St. Croix River, but she and hers were certainly there in spirit. There is a good chance that most—if not all—of Johan and Catherine's children and grandchildren made it to St. Paul and to Oakland Cemetery.

There, in a solemn gathering alongside that small hill that overlooks Jackson Street—a few hundred yards east of where rich old Henry Sibley had been buried amid much pomp and ceremony just a few months before—and beneath that beautiful grove of oak trees, Johan and Catherine and little Sarah Kochendorfer were laid to rest properly, their souls commended to their God, surrounded and attended to by their brave and loyal family.

Notes

[1]Carley, pp. 84-86. It would be weeks before Minnesotans pieced together the evidence that it had been Little Crow the farmer had killed.

[2]Oehler, p. 228.

[3]Carley, pp.78-81.

[4]Satterlee, p. 30.

[5]The Story of Mary Schwandt, Minnesota Historical Society (1894).

[6]As Sibley's troops neared Camp Release and the warriors prepared to flee, Snana worried Mary would be taken, and Snana wrote that ". . . I dug a hole inside my tent and put some poles across, and then spread my blankets over them as if nothing unusual had happened. Who do you suppose was inside my hole? My dear captive girl, Mary Schwandt, and my own two little children." Collections of the Minnesota Historical Society, Volume IX (1901), pp. 427-430.

[7]Ibid.

[8]Ibid.

[9]The Story of Mary Schwandt (1894), Minnesota Historical Society.

[10]Old Rail Fence Corners, p. 145.

[11]Satterlee, p. 30.

[12]Childhood Recollections of Old St. Paul by M. Ramsey Furness (1948), p. 123.

[13]Son Johan believed his father was born in 1824 and was, therefore, thirty-eight years old at the time of his death.

[14]This notice was translated from the German many years later by Margaret Kochendorfer.

[15]The Eberts had three children of their own, and a fourth on the way, during the winter of 1862-1863.

[16]The two of them may have known one another from before the Uprising: they probably would have attended church services and Sunday School together from late 1857 until April 1862.

[17]Book of Hebrews 12:1.

[18]Tribal leader American Horse's 1891 testimony appeared recently in the August 2012 issue of National Geographic, p. 48.

"A LASTING PEACE"

THE FOUR KOCHENDORFER children who made their way to St. Paul in September 1862 were lucky to be going to a place that offered them sanctuary, and solace, and a chance to start anew.

They were taken in by members of their church: the Feldhousers, the Van Walds, the Schmidts. The Schmidts were critical to their survival, but all of them were important, and all of them were connected to the Kochendorfers through the church.

CONSIDER MORE BROADLY the crucial role the church community of St. Paul in 1862 played in nurturing and sustaining these early settlers, and specifically these four very vulnerable Kochendorfer orphans who stepped onto the St. Paul city landing in September 1862. Civic life in Minnesota in 1862 was little more than church life; government provided only the thinnest of support structures. The church saved the lives of young Johan, Rosina, Catherine, and Margaret Kochendorfer, and provided them with the homes that allowed each of them to thrive.

In 1937, Margaret Kochendorfer wrote to the Redwood Falls Historical Society of her memories of those difficult times many years before. She described the horrific events of that fateful August day, but also recalled and emphasized the charity of Gottfried and Mary Schmidt. She wrote that in addition to the Indian child Charles in 1854 and the two Kochendorfer children in 1863 that they kept in their care, the Schmidts later took in four other children as well, and "so in this way they [the Schmidts] gave seven children good homes."[1]

The young Kochendorfers went their somewhat separate, but all very fertile and life-affirming ways. They had grown up speaking German in German farming communities, but they would grow into proud, English-speaking American citizens. As they did, their very first names would change.

Johan, who as he grew older and more proudly American began to prefer being called John, raised raspberries, strawberries, and blackberries five miles south of St. Paul, very near where he had farmed with the Schmidts. He built houses in the area, including one for his sister Catherine's family. He married Philopena Bach of nearby Woodbury, and together they had five children. He was "big brother" to his younger sisters, loaning them money in a few cases to help them get their families started.

John built a sturdy two-story Victorian-style brick house on the farmstead in the 1870s, a house that still stands proudly today. It is now surrounded by suburban ranch houses in what is now an "inner ring" suburb of St. Paul. He served on the school board and in other various civic offices, and was one of the founders of South St. Paul High School.

John and Philopena's five children had many children. The family names of their many descendants (apart from the many Kochendorfers) include Hill, Johnson, O'Malley, Verhaal, Kreuser, Hinze, Morrow, Kartes, Steele, Adams, Gerstkemper, Hopkins, Conlan, Bradshaw, Port, Johnson, Fleeger, Murray, Kortes, Lubinski, Parmalee. Many of them still live in and around St. Paul, some in Alaska and California.

One of John's granddaughters is Eileen Kochendorfer of Oakdale, Minnesota, who, at the time of this writing, was ninety-four years young. Eileen remembers Grandpa John from family events in the 1920s and early 1930s. He was a quiet man, and to Eileen's way of thinking at the time, a little old-fashioned. She remembers that Grandpa John had trouble with one arm, probably the arm that had been broken and hadn't quite healed properly during the trip from Illinois in 1857. Eileen was eight-years-old when John and Philopena celebrated their fiftieth wedding anniversary, and she remembers the gold cutlery the family bought for them. Those hard-scrabble early days never entirely left John, though. Eileen remembers that her Grandpa John kept track of and cared for the pennies, with the hope that then the dollars would take care of themselves.

John was often called upon to tell the story of those dramatic days in 1862. Eileen remembers this happened at family gatherings, often when people were done eating and the dishes were being cleared. She recalls that Grandpa John would speak of those events very quietly, staring off in the distance, almost as if he were lost in a reverie as he recalled the details all over again. He would remember again and tell how he and his sisters had to flee, and then later how difficult it was to carry five -year-old Margaret for stretches on that long August afternoon.

JOHN'S SISTER ROSINA, who later preferred Rose, must have been a very hearty, independent soul. She was the first of the children to marry, at age sixteen, in 1869, and she and her husband Theodore worked the farm in Trimbelle Township for many years. Her husband died when she was fifty-three years old, and a few years later, her children grown, Rose decided to try homesteading again . . . alone . . . in North Dakota! Family members remember Rose telling the story that, when she first got to the homestead, she slept atop her trunk, and as she nodded off she could hear the mice chewing away along the floor beneath her.

Rose did not like to dwell too much on the unfortunate events of 1862. She may have thought it an old story, or one perhaps too difficult for her children and grandchildren to hear. It had all been so very long ago, she might have said if asked about it. When she died in 1934, the obituary her descendants drew up for her did not mention the events of 1862, but instead emphasized her friends and her many children and grandchildren.

One of Rose's great-granddaughters is Judy Lindstrom of Woodbury, Minnesota. Judy grew up in Trimbelle Township, and she tells the family story that Mrs. Keller, the mother of the family farming in Trimbelle in 1862, was living with her husband and their sons. Mrs. Keller had no daughter of her own, and when she heard through her church of the calamity that had befallen the Kochendorfers, she saw the chance to acquire a daughter in young Rosina.

Judy keeps photos of her great-grandmother Rose and Rose's beautiful daughter Erma, Judy's grandmother, and of Judy's father and uncle, Rose's grandsons, in their U.S. Army uniforms as they prepared to go off to war in the 1940s. Judy is a "Baby Boomer," and Rose died long before she was born, but Judy's father had been with "Grandma Rose" when she died. Judy was curious about Grandma Rose, and her father told her that Grandma Rose was "fearless," and had a touch of "wanderlust."

Theodore and Rose Keller had six children, and their children had still more children. Family names of their many descendants include Erdmeyer, Keller, Kinkead, Lund, Kommeth, McLaughlin, Bartlett, Dosdall, Tabor, Regan, Nelson, Lennarts, Moore, Thorson, Lodemeier, Thumann, Jonas, Duden, Hauschidt, Whitcomb, Kelley, Abrams, Dosdall, Hinnenkamp, McGuire, Hurley, Pompeo, Mayer, Druck, Lennartson, Harrod, Nelson, Lindstrom, Thom, Nugent, Rief, McHardy. Many still live in western Wisconsin, many more just across the border in Minnesota.

In August 1926, Rose and John agreed to sit down with the *St. Paul Pioneer Press* newspaper for an article to be published on the sixty-fourth anniversary of the "massacres." The two of them went patiently through the events of 1862 all over again. They remembered the heroism and work-ethic of their father, the horrible screams of their mother, their weariness on reaching Beaver Creek. They were both in their seventies—it had been many years—but their memories, and their word choices, were still vivid.[2]

Their sister Catherine—by 1926, Rose referred to her as "Kate"—married Jacob Stapf of Farmington, and she outdid her sisters and brother by having twelve children (two of whom died in infancy). The many family names of her many descendants are almost too numerous to list: Stapf, Black, Manke, Phillips, Lord, Cross, Almen, Hoffman,

Yahnke, Ervasti, Betzold, Schmitz, Sprute, Luebben, Hoeppner, Ristola, Drummond, Pflaum, Simpson, Simas, Adler, Pirius, Wallin, Nighus, Bignell, Klotter, Jones, Can, Bohlen, Wille, Patrick, Anno, Brewer, Rasmussen, Cahill, Henry, Bauler, Brummund, Tutewohl, Eidness, Radman, Boykin, Covacich, Hensell, Gambrill, Hudson, Brown, Schwebeck, Peterson, Vander Plaats, Laubach, Sachen, Brava, Kephart, Halbersma, Jemiola, Roberts, Harrington, Anderson, Fillinger, Vanman, Lorenz, Juvie, and Jacobson. Catherine died in 1896, at forty-one years of age, in Farmington.

One of Catherine's descendants, granddaughter Marjorie Kathryn "Marne" Stapf, was born in 1921 in Mobridge, South Dakota. She went off to college, received a masters in Social Work from the University of Minnesota, and returned to Mobridge. There is a large Indian reservation just across the Missouri River from Mobridge, and Marne became a true friend to the Indians there. Her work with the Indians, especially the children, was recognized in a formal ceremony during which tribal leaders conferred upon her the honorary Dakotah name Wah-OH-ke-yah-WIN ("Woman Who Is Willing to Help"). The state of South Dakota, in recognition of this work, awarded her their Humanitarian Award for the year 1984.[3]

Another of Catherine's many grandchildren is Marilyn Hoffman. Marilyn lives and farms today with her husband near Hampton, Minnesota, very near the farm her grandmother went to live and work on in 1863. Marilyn has collected and maintained many of the family records.[4] She was given and has carefully kept the letters her great-grandmother wrote on settling in Minnesota to her sister back in Illinois. She keeps other family memorabilia as well, including the photo of her great uncle John and Charles Schmidt, the two adopted sons of Gottfried and Mary Schmidt.

Marilyn remembers very fondly the family reunions at great uncle John's farm, and the big front yard there where she played. Marilyn tells the family story of the day in November 1933 when family leader John, then eighty-two years old, went missing. A search of the area found him sitting with his back up against the trunk of a tree, no longer alive, but a peaceful, contented expression on his face. Life had dealt John Kochendorfer some tough breaks, but his family read in that contented expression a feeling that he had done his level best, and that "all was well."

Margaret, John's sister, the little five-year-old who fell fast asleep alongside Beaver Creek during her flight to Fort Ridgely, left the care of Mr. and Mrs. Gottfried Schmidt to marry John Erchinger in 1882. The two of them lived in St. Paul for many years and had four children. They moved to Tacoma, Washington, when Margaret was forty-one years old, and Margaret gave birth to a fifth child shortly after settling in Tacoma.

Margaret—"Maggie" in later years—began corresponding with her aunt Rosina Ebert back in Illinois in the 1880s. Her aunt was then in her fifties, but she was a wealth of information concerning the families of both Margaret's mother and her father Johan, those relatives who still resided back in Germany, in Wuerttemberg. These German relatives also wrote to Margaret. One such letter described old photographs that had been sent to Germany many years before showing then young Margaret and Mr. Gottfried Schmidt along with "his [Schmidt's] wife, a good friend and two orphans also on the photo." Margaret's

Margaret "Maggie" (Kochendorfer) Erchinger in 1886.

Aunt Rosina had probably sent this photo on to Germany in the 1860s to show the family in Wuerttemberg that Rosina's sister Catherine's orphaned children had found good homes.

Margaret's Aunt Rosina in Illinois had kept many of the letters that Margaret's mother had written Rosina from Minnesota. The true treasure in this letter exchange was the letter Rosina had received from Margaret's mother back in November 1857. Rosina had kept that beautiful, poignant letter all those years, the letter Catherine and husband Johan had written shortly after the family had settled in Minnesota, the letter that is so full of hopes and dreams.

Margaret was later given those letters, and Margaret painstakingly translated her mother's very fine but fading German handwriting. She typed up English-language translations of the letters, parts of which appear here.

Margaret read and translated that November 1857 letter, in which her mother wrote that "I feel so happy, and thankful to God, that His wisdom so arranged it, that although we are separated, we may, with pen, ink, and paper have heartfelt talks, which is especially very dear to me at this time." Margaret would have remembered how her mother spoke German to her as a child, and she could perhaps hear again how her mother would have pronounced those German words on paper. Might Margaret have felt that same thankfulness as she considered "His wisdom" in arranging things so that Margaret could—through that same medium of "pen, ink, and paper"—hear again from her beloved mother? One can hope so.[5]

Margaret would pass those letters, along with her English translations, on to other family members. Eventually they would reside with her sister Catherine's granddaughter, Marilyn Hoffman.

Rose, Maggie, and John visit sister Kate's grave.

Margaret moved to Tacoma shortly after her sister Kate died, but she stayed in close touch with her brother John and her sister Rose. She traveled back to Minnesota from Tacoma to visit with John and Rose and their families. On one of those trips back the three of them all traveled down to Farmington to visit their sister's grave. There the three of them—Rose, Maggie, and John—were photographed alongside the gravestone of their beloved sister Kate.

Margaret was the first of us to become fascinated by the Kochendorfer family genealogy, perhaps sensing even early on that the growth of the family was in some way miraculous. She kept track of and counted all those descending from her and her brother and two sisters. In 1927 she wrote that "our parents were born one hundred and one years ago. They have now one hundred and seventeen descendants; thirteen have died, leaving one hundred and four living." Great job, Margaret!

Margaret's children and grandchildren were all in attendance when Margaret and her husband John celebrated their fiftieth wedding anniversary in Tacoma in 1932. Her many descendants live today mostly in Washington State and in California. Other family names of Margaret's many descendants include Richards, Grisell, Pitzer, Dahlager, Webb, Divelbess, Gilderoy, Smith, Huston, Cwiekowski.

Margaret was the last survivor of the four children who so narrowly escaped death that day in 1862. She died in 1937. As she herself documented, at the time of her death her descendants and those of her three siblings numbered over one hundred. By the late 1980s, their descendants were counted by Minnesota historian and genealogist Robert Tegeder and Marilyn Hoffman at roughly seven hundred fifty. At the time of this writing, the descendants of those four Kochendorfer children who kept to the woods and hid in the long grass and crept so carefully and bravely to safety now number over one thousand.

I have since gone back to look at that somber gravestone in Oakland Cemetery. Now, however, I look from that stone bearing the names of father, mother, and three-year-old daughter with that sad inscription to another, identically shaped stone with the same family name on it only a few dozen yards away. There are some modest, small stones just beside the large proud family stone. I read on one of them: "John 1851-1933 Father."

Johan! Little Johan, the seven-year-old boy with the confused expression and the hair pointing every which way in the old family photograph! Young Johan, who on that dreadful day heeded his father's dying instructions to him to run for the woods, and who remembered what his father told him about the way to Fort Ridgely.

Johan, the older brother who kept his sisters concealed, and who tried to comfort them when they cried. Johan, who carried his younger sister for stretches that day when she couldn't go on. Johan, who in doing all of this dodged the grim death that the forces of history seemed to have planned for him and for his sisters. John, who in the years that followed never let those events create inside of him a hatred that might have poisoned and ruined the rest of his life. John!

I look at that small stone and suddenly this place brings to mind not sadness and death but life—Glorious Life!—and all the good that survived that difficult time.

Notes

[1] Gottfried Schmidt died in 1890. Following his death, his wife, Mary, lived with Margaret and her husband, John Erchinger. Mary lived with the Erchingers in Tacoma, Washington, until her death in 1908.

[2] *St. Paul Pioneer Press*, August 15, 1926. The full-page article, entitled "Warning Unheeded, Children See Parents Die in Indian Raid," appeared in the magazine section of the Sunday edition. The "warning" referred to was one young Johan was given by an "Indian woman" on the day before the attack. He mentioned it to his parents, but his parents ignored it, saying they had heard that some of the local settlers had taken a similar warning seriously three years before and no attack occurred.

[3] *The Kochendorfers and the Sioux Uprising* by R. Tegeder (1988).

[4] Marilyn's detailed list of Johan and Catherine's many descendants (and their spouses) runs forty-one pages, single spaced. I'm not kidding.

[5] We know that Margaret had a gift for gratitude. She closed one of her letters describing her life, her parents and her family story as follows: "The devout Christian life [of her parents] and the earnest prayers for their children have been a great blessing to us and our children. My prayer is that all the descendants may so live, taking Jesus as their Savior and guide, and that we may all meet in that heavenly home, praising God for His wonderful love shown us here."

WRITER'S POSTSCRIPT

I MADE THE DRIVE from St. Paul to Flora Township on August 18, 2012, 150 years to the day after the massacre of the Kochendorfers and the Schwandts and so many others. It was a verdant, sunny day. The rest of the country was complaining of drought conditions and poor crop yields, but I saw none of that on the drive through this "blessed plot" between St. Paul and Redwood Falls. I sat comfortably in my air-conditioned sedan, my CD player helping me enjoy the ride, and glided effortlessly by the glass office towers, the manicured golf courses.

The road I took passed south and west out of the metro area and down into the Minnesota River valley, and there I began to feel the tug of the past. Freeway signs announced the exits for Shakopee, the suburb named for Chief Shakopee, and the distance to the city of Mankato, named after Chief Mankato, two of the chiefs at the center of 1862 events.

I made the right turn at Highway 19 and drove across the Minnesota River and through the old river crossing town of Henderson. The old-fashioned store fronts on the tidy little main street there hint at a prosperity that has passed the town by—literally, passed it by on the popular Highway 169 that ignores Henderson and whisks its travelers south for St. Peter and Mankato. Henderson is the town whose citizens in November 1862 pelted and jeered the mostly innocent Indian prisoners as they made their way through the town under armed government escort from Camp Release to Fort Snelling.

The fifty-mile drive across the fertile plain that sits between the north- and the south-flowing halves of the Minnesota River, the area between Henderson and Morton, looks today like everything those early settlers could have hoped for. The corn and soybeans spring up out of the black soil right to the road's edge.

The paved road ended at Morton, and from there County Road 15 took me on gravel over Beaver Creek and then, miles later, over Middle Creek, hugging the north edge of the river valley. I looked down into the shady creek beds, through the thick tree growth that concealed the Kochendorfer children all those years ago.

Everything was so lush, so beautiful. I got out of the car and looked at the Schwandt Memorial, a sturdy stone obelisk, dedicated back in 1915, that sits alongside a simple driveway. The tendentious inscription proclaims that the unfortunate folks farming this land on August 18, 1862, were "Martyrs for Civilization."

Perhaps so. Time and study permits us to identify many others, equally innocent, who resided nearby that day and who paid with their lives as well. They were—all of them, on both sides of the Minnesota River, settlers and Indians alike—caught up in a maelstrom generated by that otherwise noble goal of growth and wealth and progress for all.

BIBLIOGRAPHY

Ambrose, Stephen. *Undaunted Courage.* New York, New York: Simon and Schuster (1997).

Anderson, G.C. and Woolworth, A.R. *Through Dakota Eyes.* St. Paul, Minnesota: Minnesota Historical Society Press (1988).

Boutin, Loren Dean. *Cut-Nose: Who Stands on a Cloud.* St. Cloud, Minnesota: North Star Press (2006).

Bryant, Charles S and Murch, Abel B. *A History of the Great Massacre by the Sioux Indians in Minnesota.* Cincinnati, Ohio: Rickey and Carroll Publishers (1864).

Buck, Solon and Elizabeth. *Stories of Early Minnesota.* New York: MacMillan Company (1925).

Carley, Kenneth. *The Great Sioux Uprising of 1862.* St. Paul, Minnesota: Minnesota Historical Society Press (1976).

Cox, Hank H. *Lincoln and the Sioux Uprising of 1862.* Nashville, Tennessee: Cumberland House (2005).

Folwell, William Watts. *A History of Minnesota.* St. Paul: Minnesota Historical Society Press (1924).

Fraker, G. *Lincoln in Woodford County* (2012).

Giesinger, Adam *From Catherine to Khruschev—The Story of Russia's Germans.* Lincoln, Nebraska: American Historical Society of Germans from Russia (1974).

Heard, Isaac V.D. *History of the Sioux War and Massacres of 1862 and 1863.* New York: Harper & Brothers (1864).

Herndon, William. *Herndon's Lincoln.* Springfield, Illinois: The Herndon's Lincoln Publishing Company (1889).

Hubbard, Lucius F. and Holcombe, Return I. *Minnesota in Three Centuries- Volume III.* New York, New York: The Publishing Society of Minnesota (1908).

Kunz, Virginia Brainard. *St. Paul–The First 150 Years.* St. Paul, Minnesota: St. Paul Foundation (1991).

Kochendorfer Family Papers and Records. Dakota County Historical Society and the private collection of Marilyn Hoffman.

Leavenworth, L. *Old Rail Fence Corners.* Austin, Minnesota: F.H. McCulloch Printing Co. (1914)

Lewis, M. and Clark, W. *Journals of the Lewis and Clark Expedition.* Washington, D.C.: National Geographic Adventure Classics (2002).

McPherson, James M. *Battle Cry of Freedom: The Civil War Era.* Oxford History of the United States (1988).

McPherson, James M. *This Mighty Scourge: Perspectives on the Civil War.* Oxford University Press (2007).

Minnesota in the Civil and Indian Wars. St. Paul, Minnesota: St. Paul Pioneer Press Co., (1890).

Myers, Jean. *Justice Served–An Essay: Abraham Lincoln and the Melissa Goings Case.* Metamora: Woodford County Courthouse site (2007).

Oehler, C.M. *The Great Sioux Uprising.* New York: Oxford Press (1959).

Ramsey, Alexander. *Diary of Alexander Ramsey*

Ramsey Furness, Marion. *Childhood Recollections of Old St. Paul.* St. Paul, Minnesota: Minnesota Historical Society Press (1948).

Reminiscences of the Sioux Outbreak. Minnesota Historical Society, Manuscripts Collections.

Sandburg, C. *Abraham Lincoln: The Prairie and the War Years.* New York, New York: Harcourt Brace and Co. (1926).

Satterlee, Marion. *Massacre by Dakota Indians.* Minneapolis: (1923).

Schwandt, M. The Story of Mary Schwandt (1894), *Collections of the Minnesota Historical Society* 6 (1894).

Snana. *"Narration of a Friendly Sioux,"* in Minnesota Historical Society Collections (1901).

Swisshelm, Jand Grey. *Half a Century.* Chicago: Jansen, McClurg and Company (1881).

Tegeder, Robert. *The Kochendorfers and the Sioux Uprising.* St. Paul, Minnesota: Robert Tegeder (1988).

Welles, Gideon. *Diary of Gideon Welles.* Boston and New York: Houghton Mifflin Company (1911).

Whipple, H.B. *Light and Shadows of a Long Episcopate: Being Reminiscences and Recollections of the Right Reverend Henry Benjamin Whipple, Bishop of Minnesota.* New York: MacMillan Company (1899).

Whipple, H.B. *The Duty of Citizens Concerning the Indian Massacre*

INDEX

Pike, Captain Zebulon, 6, 7, 15.
Pine Ridge Reservation (South Dakota), 108.
Pope, Major General John, 75, 76, 82, 83, 85, 88, 94, 101.
Ramsey, Alexander, 6, 67, 70, 71, 88, 91, 100-102.
Rdainyanka (Rattling Runner), 79.
Reconstructionist, 101.
Red Middle Voice, 41, 43, 49-53, 59, 81, 95.
Red River of the North, 7.
Redwood Falls, Minnesota, viii, 111, 121.
Redwood River, 34.
Release, Camp, 78, 79, 82, 94, 95, 97, 101, 102, 120.
Renville Rangers, 67, 68.
Republican Party, 18, 21, 26, 40.
Rice Creek, 31, 36, 50, 51, 72.
Rice, Henry M., 87.
Riggs, Reverend Stephen, 78, 79.
Roessler family and farm, 95.
Sacagawea, 28.
Santee Indians, 97.
Schmidt, Charles, 104, 105, 115.
Schmidt, Gottfried, 12, 103-105, 107, 111, 113, 115, 116.
Schmidt, Mary, 103, 105, 111, 115, 116.
Schwandt, August, 59, 71, 95.
Schwandt, Johan, 36, 37, 59, 60, 95, 120.
Schwandt, Mary, 36, 45, 46, 50, 59, 76, 96, 97.
Scott, General Winfield, 41.
Seder, Reverend Louis, 51, 60.
Shakopee, Chief, 31, 45, 49, 52, 70, 120.
Shawnee Indians, 29.
Sheehan, Lieutenant Timothy68, 70.
Shiloh, Tennessee, 41.
Sibley, Henry Hastings, 5, 8, 14-16, 70, 71, 74-79, 81, 83, 84, 88, 95, 97, 100, 101, 109.
Sioux Indians, 5-7, 14, 15, 28, 31, 42, 45, 47, 50, 52, 53, 76-78, 83, 87, 98, 104.
Sisseton Indians, 6, 77, 80.
Sitting Bull, 109.
Snana (Maggie Brass), 96, 97.
Soldiers' Lodge, Rice Creek, 31, 50, 77.

St. Croix River
St. Paul Pioneer Press, 114.
St. Paul, Minnesota, vii-ix, 5, 7, 10, 11, 13-17, 27, 32-35, 37, 55, 67, 70, 71, 74, 75, 78, 95-97, 100-104, 106, 108, 109, 111-114, 116, 120.
St. Peter, Minnesota, 67, 68, 72, 74, 75, 101, 120.
Stanton, Secretary of War Edwin M., 83.
Stapf, Jacob, 106, 114.
Stapf, Marjorie Kathryn "Marne," 115.
Stevenson, Adlaid, 3.
Sturgis, Private William, 66, 67, 70.
Swisshelm, Jane Grey, 83, 84, 86, 102, 106.
Tacoma, Washington, 116, 117.
Taylor, President Zachary, 6.
Timms, Henry, 106, 108.
Treaty of Mendota, 5, 6.
Treaty of Traverse des Sioux, 5-7, 101.
Trimbelle Township, Wisconsin, 104, 106, 109, 113, 114.
Upper Agency (Yellow Medicine), 47, 77.
Von Wald, Reverend and Mrs., 103, 104.
Wahpekute Indians, 6.
Wahpeton Indians, 6, 80.
Wakanajaja (George Crooks), 82.
Walz, Caroline Schwandt, 98.
Welles, Secretary of the Navy Gideon, 83.
Whipple, Bishop Henry Benjamin, 5, 28-30, 44, 45, 85-87, 100.
Wilkinson, Morton S., 88.
Wilson, Clara, 50.
Wood Lake (Minnesota), Battle of, 77.
Woodford County, Illinois, 2-4, 8, 20, 33, 102.
Wounded Knee Creek (South Dakota), 109.
Wounded Knee, South Dakota, 109.
Wuerttemberg, Germany, 2, 103, 116.

Marilyn Hoffman with the author, showing her family records.